I0616985

TIMEWALKER

THOMAS F. MONTELEONE

JOURNALSTONE
YOUR LINK TO ARTIST TALENT

ISBN: 978-1-68510-031-5 (sc)
ISBN: 978-1-68510-032-2 (ebook)
Library of Congress Catalog Number: 2022931586

First printing edition: March 18, 2022
Published by JournalStone Publishing in the United States of America.
Cover Design: Freer Law | Interior Photo: Zack Frank
Edited by Sean Leonard
Proofreading and Cover/Interior Layout by Scarlett R. Algee

JournalStone Publishing
3205 Sassafras Trail
Carbondale, Illinois 62901

JournalStone books may be ordered through booksellers or by contacting:
JournalStone | www.journalstone.com

*This one is for
my handsome, son, Damon
and
my beautiful daughter, Olivia
(you can't beat good genes!)*

TIMEWALKER

1

"I'VE GOT SOME BAD news, Doc." The cowboy named Zeke Hardesty looked at Edward Drinker Cope with an expression equal parts sadness and trepidation, then turned his head to spit out a large black blob of tobacco juice.

"And what might that be?" Edward had been sitting by the evening campfire, sipping the last of his bitter coffee while the sun began to hide behind the distant Black Hills at his back. His sketchbook lay by his side on a flat rock. It was his favorite time of the day other than those special and magical moments when he discerned a fossilized bone disguised within a shelf of limestone or shale.

"Henry Dawkins—looks like he ain't gonna be our guide no more..."

Edward looked up at Zeke with a sudden increased interest. "What? Why not?"

The cowboy maneuvered the chaw into his cheek, then rubbed the rough stubble of his beard as though the gesture might help get his words out. "Well, sir, on account of he didn't come back last night."

Edward considered this, and was not certain this necessarily meant Dawkins would not be returning at some point. He had driven the expedition's freight wagon full of specimen crates to the rail station at Cheyenne – about four and a half days' ride there and back.

"It's possible he has been delayed," said Edward. "He could come riding in at any time now."

"I don't reckon that's gonna be happenin'...on account me and Harley went out lookin' for him this afternoon when he didn't show last night and..." Zeke paused as if the words were getting caught in his mouth.

"And *what,* man?!" Edward dumped the dregs of his coffee into the dirt by the fire, stood to face his employee. "Get on with it! And *what?*"

"...and we found Henry still half-sittin' up in the supply wagon with a tomahawk stickin' outta his head and his scalp freshly took..."

The words pierced him like a savage's arrow. He was suddenly aware of the slowly diminishing heat of the day as it lingered in the surrounding rock formations. And despite the temperatures, he felt a brief chill. Henry Dawkins had been a good young man. Fresh out of the Army, he knew the Dakota and Montana Territories better than most. In addition, he'd been a good scout of possible excavation sites as well as an expert in getting them safely from place to place in such inhospitable environs. How had he become so careless as to be ambushed by hostiles?

"Oh, no..." said Edward, but no other words would come.

"The Blackfeet, I figures. Although it could be Lakota Sioux. Not that it matters in the long run." Another hock and launch of another black globule.

"Where did you find him?"

"'Bout six miles back along the stage route. That's where we buried 'im. Right along there. Oh, and they took the horses too."

His stomach suddenly churning, Edward felt as if he might discharge the beans and hardtack from supper. He felt a bit lightheaded as well. Of course the Indians had taken the horses, and they would be expensive to replace. He hated the idea of telegraphing Philadelphia for additional funds. If they thought he was mis-managing his budget, this might be his last sponsored sojourn into fossil country.

"What about the wagon?"

Zeke spit again. "Looked plenty okay to me. We hauled it back in about two hours ago. We gave it to Mr. Sternberg. He's checking it out to be sure."

"That's good, at least." Edward had been wondering where George Sternberg had been keeping himself. Usually, his right-hand man and fellow paleontologist did not require much time to ensure all the horses were fed and secured for the night. "Thank you, Zeke."

"Jes' doin' my job." Another black blob began to seep from between his brown teeth as he managed a weak smile, then half-turned to go. "I guess I'll be settlin' in for the night. Good night, Doc."

"One more moment, if you please." Edward held up his index finger as if ready to make a point. "What are we going to do without a guide?"

Zeke turned back to regard him, his smile no longer gracing his unshaven face. "I suppose we could consider ourselves fairly well fucked...or me and Harley could head up to the Black Hills Depot and try to find us another one."

Edward had no idea if they could make that happen. Dawkins had been referred to him as a result of a letter of introduction from the Philadelphia Academy of Natural Sciences sent to a General Haverson at Fort Bridger in Wyoming. Haverson arranged for Edward to meet Dawkins in Cheyenne after the young corporal had been recently cashiered out. It had all gone so smoothly, Edward had not given the idea of ever needing another guide a second thought.

Zeke stood there looking at him as if waiting to be dismissed.

Edward addressed him. "They have guides there? Waiting around to be hired?"

"Not a-zackly, but I know some of the Shoshone Tribe come through the depot to trade goods. They're right peaceful Injuns. They are."

"So I am aware," said Edward.

It was 1876 and Edward had been traveling into the American West in search of his precious fossils every year since 1872. During that time, he had evolved from his initial terror at the very mention of the word "Indian" to a comfortable knowledge and understanding of the various tribes, their customs, their intentions toward the white men gradually subsuming their lands, and their likelihoods of ever bringing harm to him or his expeditions. Occupying a small portion in the southwest corner of Montana, the Shoshone were known more for their hunting and agrarian pursuits than their talent for making war. Their relations with the white man and the United States Army had been almost universally amicable, and since Edward had no experience with any of them as guides, he would have to take the word of one of his trail-beaten hired hands.

"Very well then. Can you dispatch yourselves to the depot in the morning?"

Zeke rubbed the uneven ginger-brown growth along his jaw that could hardly be called a beard. "Sure, I reckon, but does that mean we get some bonus money for takin' the risk?"

Edward let a heavy breath escape him without it becoming a full blossomed sigh. He wished he'd never promised his band of rowdies any such thing as risk pay, because he'd honestly believed they were beyond risk. Most of the tribes in this region of the Territories either knew Edward Drinker Cope, the bone-hunter, or they'd heard tales of him. For the most part, they left him to his odd, and what they found to be silly, pursuits. Other than certain factions of the Sioux, the hostility of the various tribes seemed to be on the wane – at least that was Edward's firm belief. In fact, his encounter with a large band of marauding Sioux had become something of a legend in these parts.

…While digging in the Badlands, Edward's camp had been invaded by a fierce brace of Lakota warriors on horseback. But they did not attack, because their leader, a tall muscular brave named Nehoma, had taken immediate notice of Cope's men in the process of fully exposing the skull of a predatory carnivore he suspected may be another specimen of the *laelaps* he'd originally discovered in New Jersey. Emerging from the limestone like a wraith taking solid form, the creature's huge eye sockets and impossibly sharp teeth were impossible to ignore. Nehoma had clearly never seen anything like it and expressed a mixture of fascination and fear. It had been the kind of distraction that could turn the entire dangerous situation around.

Realizing this, Cope had seized upon the moment to give the savage a quick lesson regarding the burgeoning field of paleontology. He spoke through his guide, a half-breed who knew the rudimentaries of several of the region's Indian dialects. In the intervals between the verbal exchanges, Edward dug out his large sketch pad from his saddlebag and showed Nehoma page after page of detailed and skillful drawings of what some of the dinosaurs might have looked like *in vivo*. While initially transfixed, the leader, however, had soon lost interest in the rarified and difficult-to-translate details, and as he began to make threatening gestures, Edward stepped forward, waving his arms and speaking in a nervous, high-pitched voice. So animated and excited had he become in an effort to speak quickly and firmly, that his false teeth went flying from his mouth.

The effect of this unexpected event created a collective gasp amongst the warriors, including Nehoma, as they stared dumbstruck at the man's teeth lying at their feet. Edward did not hesitate as he scooped up his teeth and held them up to the Indian leader, clacking them in his hand like a pair of castanets. It was a trick he had done many times for his daughter when she had been very young, much to her delight. Nehoma's stupefaction shattered as he burst into tentative laughter – an action that encouraged the remainder of his band to do the same. As the wave of mirth subsided, Edward sensed a tinge of apprehension, if not outright fear, in the cadre of painted and feathered demons. They had not been sure how to accept what they had seen him do. Perhaps he was a shaman or at least a medicine man among the white men?

With a theatrical flair, he had replaced his false teeth into his mouth, opened his eyes wide and bulging, then raised both arm like the risen Christ. "Behold!"

With that, the band of warriors began backing up their steeds, looking to Nehoma for guidance. The leader spoke to Edward's guide and, after a fairly length exchange, reared his horse into a tight turn and rode off into the advancing dusk. His minions quickly followed, leaving Edward to make what he could of the encounter by questioning his half-breed.

Bemused and apprehensive, Nehoma had asked if the white man possessed special magic, and being no fool, his guide had said yes, most definitely. He had also assured the Indian leader that Edward only used his powers in the pursuit of knowledge and would not bring harm to the land or the tribes. It had been as Edward suspected, and he thanked God that such a buffoonish mistake had actually turned out to be the salvation of his men, himself, and his expedition...

As Edward pulled himself out of the memory, he could see Zeke, still standing before him, hands on hips. "Well, Doc... Whatcha say? We gonna get some – what's the Army call it? – 'hazard pay'?"

"I have heard it called that, yes."

"Yes? You mean yes-we're-gonna-get-some? That kinda 'yes'?"

Staring up at the darkening sky, he saw the first stars and the planet Venus beginning to puncture the firmament with their pinpoints of light. A soft breeze was picking up from the east, and the heat of the day was quickly leaching itself from the surrounding rocks and bluffs.

Finally, after a long reflective pause, Edward regarded his raggedy cowboy. "All right, I'll get you an extra two dollars per day that you're on the trail. Provided you find us a new guide. No guide, no dollars."

"Deal. I'll tell Harley we ride at dawn." Zeke grinned his crooked yellow teeth, adjusted his dusty hat over his long hair, and headed for the circle of bedrolls that surrounded the expedition's nightly campfire.

"One more thing," said Edward.

Zeke stopped in mid-stride, unable to hide his eye-roll. Edward didn't care. He knew his hired men all thought of him as a typical eccentric, and that was fine as long as they bent to their work. "Yeah, Doc?"

"Can you take a letter from me to my wife? They have mail service to Denver from the depot, do they not?"

"Well, I ain't a-zackly the letter-writin' type, so I can't say for certain, but I would reckon so since it's on the stage line."

"Very good. Stop and see me in the morning before your departure, and I shall give you my missive."

"Huh? I thought you said a letter..."

"I meant— No...never mind you. Just...see me in the morning."

2

June 15, 1876
My Dearest Anne:

I TRUST YOU AND our precious daughter are safe and happy in the thriving city of Denver. Despite your original misgivings of traveling there to wait out my work, I have hopes that you have grown to like what is fast becoming a real city. Its days as a grubby gold mining settlement are long gone, and while I suspect it still lacks the cultural and culinary delights of our beloved Philadelphia, I pray it complementary enough to keep you and Julia agreeably diverted.

I am sorry my correspondence is spotty at best, but as we traverse the Territories, the opportunity to post a letter remains scant. When circumstances required me to send one of my men to the Black Hills Depot, I did not forgo the chance to send this hastily scribed letter to let you know that I am safe. You can also rejoice in the knowledge that our relentless hunt for bones has rewarded us with some magnificent specimens of both known creatures and exciting new and yet-to-be categorized (and named) beasts. The longer I forage for their remains, the more I stand in awe of the grandiosity of nature and its power to produce such spectacular fauna!

George Sternberg, fresh from the campus of KSU, has proved an assistant to me, and as time proceeds, he is becoming to me something of which I have few: a friend. He exhibits not only loyalty and dedication to his avocation, but also a genuine warmth. He is an optimist in all things and the smile that usually defines his features is a welcome sight in this harsh and unforgiving land of southwest Montana. His knowledge of horses and carpentry has been an incalculable bonus, and I have invested my total trust in his abilities.

In addition, we've seen no signs of Marsh and his band of rowdies. There is talk of him roaming the escarpments eighty miles to our north and farther east into the Dakotas, but there is no way to substantiate it. If true, he is sufficiently away from our current operations to represent not even the slightest of threats.

We find ourselves deep into the Judith River basin, and my instincts tell me this is a fossil-rich area just waiting for my pick and my brush. It is a wild and uninhabited land. I do not say that to remind you, or in any way fan the flames of your fears regarding the Indians in these Territories. The risks are not as grave as you may have heard. In fact, if the rumors I've encountered are in any way true, the most fierce of the tribes – the Sioux and the Cheyenne – are fully engaged east of here with a large detachment of U. S. Army troops that will keep them well occupied for the remainder of the summer and autumn. Besides, my reputation among the Lakota Sioux is that of a harmless and quite hapless magician.

Realizing my news is of the most dreary type, so full of mentions of my relentless tasks, I long to hear news of you and Julia – your thoughts and joys and pursuits and discoveries in your new environs. I believe the best plan would be to send your reply in care of General Delivery post office at the Cheyenne rail depot. If all goes well, our expedition will be there within two fortnights to acquire supplies for the final six weeks of the year's agreeable seasons. When that period is at its end, I shall send for you by telegraph from Cheyenne. Upon your arrival from Denver we shall board the Union Pacific for the journey back east.

The days are long here, but the nights are longer still. Each evening I am reminded ever more pointedly how much I miss your presence beside me. I pray your feelings mirror my own, and I am counting the days till I can hold you in my arms.

Until that moment, I remain
Your loving husband,
Edward

He re-read the letter once and, satisfied, folded the thick, crisp stationery to fit into its matching envelope. While he did not believe his words were in any way false or misleading, he knew they were, at their core, a bit hollow. In all his dealings, Edward strove to be an honest man. His Quaker upbringing all but guaranteed that quality deep within him, and it forced him to be equally forthright with himself. And thus he knew in his heart that while he truly loved his wife and daughter, they did not instill in him either the passion or the attention he felt every day engaged in his search for fossils.

He knew Annie suspected as much, although she'd never felt emboldened enough to confront him directly. To her it was a question she most likely feared the answer to. She knew Edward well enough to realize he was not capable of lying to her. He prayed that she never asked.

He hadn't always felt a distance from her and her city society manners, but once he'd ventured off the east coast and roamed the untamed Territories of the West, everything changed for him. As if the proverbial scales fell away from his eyes, he realized his scholarly work had not actually been *living* as much as merely existing. Out here, in the badlands and in the shadow of the Black Hills, he became aware of the fragility of life. His presence in such an unforgiving land challenged him without surcease to do just one simple, primal thing: *survive.*

And it became like an elixir to him! Never had he felt so completely *alive*. The simple joy of coming upon a fresh, clean pool of spring water, of cooking that evening's dinner on an open fire, of spotting that single aberration in the face of a cliff or mound that signaled the remnant of some great and terrible beast.

All that, he mused, while operating under the ever-present penumbra of an attack by savages or, perhaps worse, a calculated and meddling intervention by Marsh and his hooligans.

3

"YOU UP YET, DOC?"

From outside Edward's tent, the words penetrated the fog of his restless slumber and he forced himself awake.

"I am now," he said.

Zeke cleared his throat. "We're gettin' ready to head out, and you told me to—"

"Yes, yes. I know – the letter. Give me a moment."

Grabbing his sketchbook, Edward retrieved the sealed envelope addressed to Mrs. Anne Cope. Still attired in only his long johns, he exited the tent to greet the two cowpokes.

"Here you are," he said as he handed off the letter to Zeke. "Take good care to see it delivered."

Zeke turned to tuck it into his saddlebag, then buckled it shut. "Got it right'chere. Ain' goin' nowhere. Don't you fret none, Doc."

"Thank you both, gentlemen. Godspeed."

"We'll be back as soon as we can." Zeke winked, touched the brim of his hat, then let fly with a glob of tobacco juice. "Wouldn't wanna lose out on that extra pay now, would we?"

Sighing softly, Edward replied. "No, no… I suppose you would not. Now please, off with you."

Edward watched them ride off to the east, then relieved himself among the nearby rocks. The morning air felt crisp and dry, lacking the oppressive heat yet to come. As he dressed and pulled on his boots, he heard the first bangings and clangings of Charles Thibodeaux as he began breakfast preparations for everyone. He smiled and smoothed his bushy mustache as he anticipated the inventive and delicious offerings of the Frenchman.

The first year Edward had gone west with a ragtag crew of cowboys and laborers, he hadn't seen the need to budget for a real cook, figuring every man would be able to take care of his own vittles. That decision had proved almost disastrous. Some of the men had been capable hunters and provided game for themselves, while others proved helpless and hopeless to acquire enough food to sustain themselves. Hunger can do strange things to a man, Edward discovered. Stealing and sneaking off with another's provisions became the order of the day for those who could not feed themselves. Disputes and vicious fights abounded.

His trip into Kansas appeared positively doomed until Edward encountered a Chinaman by the name of Wan Soo. He was selling bags of rice and hardtack at the Topeka steamboat landing, and Edward was struck by his excellent command of English. Soon a conversation ensued, and when the man claimed to be a serviceable cook, Edward hired him on the spot. It changed everything, and the Cope Expedition soon uncovered a magnificently preserved skeleton of an elasmosaur that had roamed the inland waters of the great Kansas Sea more than 75 million years ago.

Edward was pulled from his memories by the approach of Thibodeaux carrying a tin cup of fresh-brewed coffee. "Here ya go, Perfesser," he said. "Come to the wagon when you're ready. Got some rabbit on the skillet and some rice balls."

"Thank you, Charles. I will be there shortly."

Accepting the coffee, Edward held it in both hands, letting its warmth drive away the stiffness in his digits. Already he was suffering from the early stages of arthritis, most likely brought on by the long days of chunking off pieces of rock with small hammers and picks. His wife and colleagues at the university often chastised him for his penchant for getting down in the dirt to dig. It was not fit work for an educated man, a man of means, they said. Better left to his laborers, they said.

Edward grinned as he recalled such dismissive comments and also the summary response in the tobacco-chaw-stained words of Zeke Hardesty: *Fuck them!*

He gulped down half the cup, then stood up and headed for the chuck wagon. George Sternberg, already in line with a tin plate in hand, nodded in greeting. He was a short, stocky man, with a thick mustache and round spectacles, who always wore a black bowler hat in preference to Edward's more traditional cowboy Stetson.

"Morning, Professor. Hope you're feeling well."

"That I am, and thank you for the inquiry."

Sternberg gestured towards the high sky. "Looks like the weather is holding. No rain, no dust storms. Another fruitful day."

"Agreed. Your students seem to be enjoying the work."

Sternberg nodded as he allowed Thibodeaux to fill his plate, then turned to Edward. "I'm not sure I would say they're exactly 'enjoying' it, but they appreciate the importance of their task and their place in the history of paleontology. That's what defines a special student, wouldn't you say?"

"Without question, George. Without question," said Edward. He picked up a plate and approached the French cook, who larded his dish with an agreeable-looking arrangement of meat and rice. He followed Sternberg to a pair of camp chairs where they sat in the shade of the rising hills to the south.

"Sad news about young Dawkins," he said as he dug his fork into the first chunk of rabbit.

"A shock to be sure." Sternberg shook his head slowly. "I liked that boy."

"We're going to need a replacement if we expect to work our way west into the other fields." Edward knocked back the rest of his coffee. "Zeke seemed to think he can find a capable soul at the depot."

"Zeke's sometimes a bullslinger, you know."

Edward grinned. "Aren't they all? All these hard-cases we hire every season…"

"Maybe so, but we've had to depend on them, haven't we?"

Edward looked at him. "Does that mean you think our party's in jeopardy?"

George scooped up the last remnants on his plate, eased it into his mouth, then chewed thoughtfully. "Well, we *could* be if we don't get a guide we can trust. And trust is what survival is all about out here. We may *think* we know this Territory, but we are being disingenuous, my friend."

"That doesn't sound like the optimist I have come to know." Edward looked off toward the trail leading from the camp.

Ignoring the comment, Sternberg tapped him on the arm. "How long do you figure before Zeke and Harley get back?"

"At least two or three days, I would imagine. The depot's more than a day's ride. And I fear it's too much to assume they might engage the services of a scout the minute they reached the settlement."

Sternberg nodded.

Edward finished the last of his rice ball. Then: "A more realistic view places their return within a week's time."

"Well," said Sternberg. "It's fortunate we still have plenty of work to do at our current location." He inclined his head and gazed toward a large sloping canyon wall rich in sedimentary layers of shale and sandstone, the types of exposures that proved excellent potential beds for fossils.

"You're right about that. Should I provide you and your students an extra pair of hands today?"

"Not yet. Let me see how we progress by mid-day. You would probably do better to check out the nearby landscapes ahead."

Edward understood Sternberg's strategy. Finding the proper locations for a fruitful dig required quiet patience in the saddle under a hard sun, scanning the outcropping of rocks, the broken faces of hills and scarps. A careless eye could easily miss that tiny singular irregularity that signaled a fossil waiting to be found.

"Very well, I'll head out soon before the sun's too high."

Sternberg stood, returned to the chuck wagon, and handed his empty plate and cup to Thibodeaux.

Edward joined him. "Any idea yet what type of creature you've uncovered?"

Sternberg rubbed his chin with the back of his hand. "Not sure yet. I reckon we've got two different specimens close by each other. After five days, we're just about ready to remove the leg bones of the bigger animal – still unidentified, although I suspect it is a biped of some medium size."

"And the other bones?"

Sternberg shrugged. "Much smaller, more delicate. I am thinking either a small theropod like the *Compsognathus* they found in Germany, or…some type of pterosaur."

"So close together…" Edward mused. "Odd *in situ* placement, unless this location had been a watering hole or a swamp where a variety of species came to drink or became trapped in some primordial ooze."

"A tar pit, perhaps. I can see that making sense. God, I wish there were some way for us to truly look back down the corridor of time to know for certain what we now can only surmise."

"That, dear George, is exactly that: a wish, and nothing more."

Sternberg glanced at his pocket watch. "Speaking of time. It is *time* to get to work. Good luck among the rocks, Professor."

"Thank you, sir. I'll get my gear and be off."

Edward headed back to his tent where he gathered up his canteen, spyglass, and his Colt six-shooter. He considered the progress of Sternberg's excavations, and found it doubtful they would be completed before Zeke and Harley's return. It could go well, or it could go poorly. Such were the vicissitudes of uncovering bones from sedimentary rock.

His horse awaited him, tied up to the wheel of one of their freight wagons, already weighed down by several crates of bones carefully wrapped in Sternberg's formula of over-cooked rice paste. It was quite ingenious – when the paste hardened it formed a formidable protective shell around the fragile fossils, making them safer for the arduous journey back east by stage, wagon, or railway car.

Checking his saddlebags for emergency hardtack, rope, and an extra canteen, Edward climbed aboard the old roan. While not an expert horseman, he had learned the rudiments of riding a steed, and remained certain dear Annie would be astonished to see him in the saddle, cowboy hat shading his dark, shaggy hair from the sun.

Giving the rains a gentle snap, Edward felt his horse swing into motion and assume a slow but steady gait along the wide banks of the Judith.

4

AN HOUR PASSED WITH Edward making frequent stops to examine questionable formations among rocks. On occasion, a potential anomaly warranted a closer look with his spyglass, or even an on-foot investigation if the object of his curiosity did not reside too high into a cliff or canyon declivity. He paused often to sketch out landmarks in the surrounding terrain, so that upon return he and his party would be able to re-locate the places he imagined may be hiding the bones of an earlier age.

Straying farther from the river basin, he headed toward a natural break in the foothills that led up and then through a narrow canyon. Lacking a true trail, the footing for his horse lacked good purchase – lots of jagged rocks and loose smaller stones. Edward pulled up the reins to pause as he considered whether or not this particular route into the box canyon was a wise choice. Not only was the going more than a bit rough, but he noticed the canyon appeared to have only one way in or out. He knew from his years out in these Territories that it would be a treacherous place to be if he encountered any hostile Indians.

No sense in being foolish, especially since he had no idea whether or not the area might yield anything of value. Turning his horse around, Edward retreated to safer ground with the intention to follow the Judith and scan its steep banks for any interesting-looking formations.

That was when he heard the animal sounds.

A chorus of high-pitched barks and yips, punctuated by aggressive growls. Edward recognized them – coyotes. Not as dangerous as a wolf, and normally afraid enough of men to keep their distance. His horse seemed to know this as well, and she wasn't reacting with trepidation. As he followed the river around a wide sweeping bend bordered by a sloping wall of crumbling rock that had to be perhaps thirty feet or so above his head, the sounds of the yipping and barking grew louder.

And now he could see why. Four coyotes pranced and darted around something lying at the base of the slope. Something darker than the surrounding colors of sienna and various shades of white and pale reds. A fallen animal perhaps. He reined his horse, and reached back into his saddlebag for his spyglass.

Even with his brass instrument, he knew he was still at a considerable distance from the beasts and whatever lay there attracting their attention – distance enough to cause the image of the dark figure to shimmer slightly as the heat in the rocks steadily increased under the unforgiving glare of the sun. But there was enough definition to tell him it looked like the body of a man, still and unmoving.

No wonder the coyotes were excited; perhaps they had recently encountered their next meal.

"Come on, girl… Let's go have a look."

A quick snap of the reins and he was moving forward along the rough bank, and soon Edward became convinced his initial assessment had been correct. Lying at the base of a gradual slope of scree, a human lay on its side and had not moved amidst the cacophony of the coyote pack.

Closer still, and Edward saw the features of a buckskin tunic and headband resolve themselves. He did not need a look through the spyglass to know he looked upon a fallen Indian, and there was no telling from what tribe he might be. His first inclination was to keep up his approach at a wary pace. He could feel himself sweating into his hatband and knew it was more from anxiety than the rising heat of the day.

What was going on here? Replacing his spyglass to his bag, he lifted his Colt from its stiff holster, and placed his index finger to rest gently on the trigger.

He pulled up when he was no closer than thirty yards of the Indian and the band of scavengers surrounding him. The animals paused in their barks and yips to all stare at rider and horse, but they showed no inclination to be run off.

"Hello there! Hello! Are you hurt?"

No reply. And then the coyotes began yipping again.

"Can you hear me?" He yelled the words, competing with the noises of the pack.

The Indian did not answer, but just then one of the beasts grew bold enough to dash up and take a nip at the figure's outstretched arm. He appeared to move slightly, shifting away from the attempted bite. *He's alive!* The motion galvanized Edward. He had to *do* something!

The movement had excited the coyotes to a new level, and the first one's tentative attack inspired the three others as they were all lunging and snapping at the fallen man. Edward's horse back-stepped a few feet, suddenly wary and becoming skittish.

"Hey!" Edward yelled as he sat astride the roan, and he raised the revolver and pointed it at the closest beast. Rather than squeezing the trigger gently and gradually as Zeke had schooled him, he yanked hard and the Colt thundered off a shot high and wide of the coyote. The boom of the report echoed faintly off a distant canyon wall as the pack moved almost as one and scurried off down the bank towards the river.

Edward smiled. Not bad. Only one shot and the threat was alleviated. He allowed himself a very brief moment to feel good about himself and how he'd handled the encounter. But there was still the matter of the savage lying ahead of him.

"Come on, girl…easy now." He holstered the six-shooter, then gave a gentle tap of his boot against the roan's flank and he was again advancing slowly, all the while scanning the basin in all directions for any sign of movement from the predating scavengers.

Dismounting by the fallen man, Edward grabbed his canteen and knelt by him. "Can you hear me?"

He reached down with one hand and touched the Indian's shoulder, moving him carefully onto his back then lifting his head. He was a fairly old man, his long hair streaked with lots of silvery gray, bound into two ponytails over each ear and held in place by a maroon headband. As Edward placed the canteen's open spout on the man's cracked lips and seeped a bit of water into his mouth, his eyes fluttered open. Suddenly a dark and fathomless gaze seemed to go right through Edward like a bullet.

The effect was more than a bit startling… He had not expected it. "Drink," he said. "That's it."

The old Indian sipped rather than gulped the water, taking his time. He managed to prop himself up on one elbow, and attempted a small lopsided smile. "Thank you," he said.

Another moment to be startled. "You…you speak English, do you?"

"Some."

"Are you hurt bad?"

"I…not know. Fall. From…" He looked up toward the zenith of the rock wall.

Edward looked up. Even with slope, that would have been a horrific tumble. The man was lucky to be alive.

"Horse scare by…"

He grasped for the word, made an undulating gesture with his hand.

"A snake!" Edward repeated the gesture.

"Yes, that word."

Pointing towards the man's head, Edward spoke. "Your *head*? You all right? You were unconscious."

The Indian looked at him uncomprehending.

Edward mimed being knocked in the head, closing his eyes and tilting his head.

The Indian allowed a small grin. "Yes. That word. Better now. Thank to you." He maneuvered himself into a sitting position, cross-legged. For an older man, he showed himself to be surprisingly limber and strong. "You save me. Coyote want eat me. In way…my life…now your."

Edward thought he understood what the man was saying, that he was in Edward's debt in some way. He extended his right hand to shake, touched his chest with his left.

"Edward. I am Edward Cope."

The Indian took the proffered hand. "I am *Hissha Bilitaachila*…but white men call me Red Moon."

Edward allowed himself a soft chuckle. "I think I shall do the same."

The Indian nodded.

"What were you doing out here? Hunting?"

"Hunting, yes, but not for animal. For plants."

"Plants?" Edward gestured out across the harsh landscape. "Not many plants out here."

"Yes. If you…know…where look."

"As I'm sure you do. What you need them for? Are you a cook? For food?"

Red Moon shook his head. "No, for my...my mixes. My special things. I am what white men call a 'medicine man.' But I am called *dappiish* in my tribe."

"Ah, I see. You use the plants to make potions and things like that?"

The Indian chanced a small grin. "Something like that."

"Also, I've been meaning to ask you..." Edward pointed at the few feathers woven into his ponytailed hair. "What *is* your tribe?"

"Crow."

Hearing that, Edward inwardly relaxed a bit. From the campfire tales of his hired hands, he had learned bits and pieces about the tribes in the Montana and Wyoming Territories. Thus he knew which ones were the most dangerous – such as the Sioux and the Cheyenne – and which were more amenable to living peacefully with the Americans. The Crow fell generally into the latter category, mainly because of the decrees of their chief, Plenty Coup, who foresaw much bloodshed and misery if his people put on their warpaint against the armies of the white man.

"Where you learn my tongue? My English?"

"Sometimes we trade. Fort Laramie. Some work for soldiers."

"You speak well." Edward offered him more water, which he accepted.

"More to talk. I be...better."

"I understand. Can I help you back to your people?"

"No. If I find horse..."

"I can help you do that as well."

Edward stood up, extended a hand to help his companion to his feet. He felt immediately comfortable around this Indian. The way he spoke, his general demeanor suggested someone of intelligence and a gentleness of spirit. It would be un-Christian to refer to him as a *savage* because he was certainly not that. There was no way to discern his true age. While his face might be defined by creases and lines, it did not reflect frailty or any lack of fortitude. He seemed a man who exuded a subtle confidence and much ability.

"I would...like. You a good man, Edward Cope."

Edward smiled, smoothed out his mustache. "Well, I try to be. I thank you, sir."

With that, they approached the roan and Edward helped Red Moon up to the saddle before setting off in search of the Indian's horse. They moved off the basin and up along a gradually rising plateau. Red Moon expressed a quiet confidence that his horse would not stray far. He intimated that the animal had been with him for many years and the attachment between man and beast had been strongly forged.

After an hour or so, as the sun rose higher and higher and grew ever hotter, Edward could feel it beating down on the back of his neck. He had been walking alongside the roan so that Red Moon might gather his strength, but the uneven terrain and the high harsh sun at mid-day had become challenging.

Taking respite under the shade of an outcropping of sandstone, the two men sat for a spell and shared the canteen. They had been talking sporadically as they searched and Edward noticed Red Moon had been correct – his English steadily improved the more he employed it.

Now he stood, stared off into the distance of the sere landscape, as if seeing something Edward could not. "This not good. Search too long."

"I am all right with it," said Edward.

"No. I first think easy to find horse..." He twittered his fingers to mimic walking. "This way."

Edward removed his hat, combed his hand through his hair. "I would say we don't have much choice in that matter."

"You do not. I *do*." Red Moon tuned and regarded Edward with an expression that could only be termed serious or possibly reproachful. "You...must...stay here. I return...with horse."

He resettled his hat, stood up to join the Indian. "No, I want to help."

"You can no help what I do now."

"But—"

"You stay here. Rest. Sleep. I go. Alone. Please."

Edward could not help but notice the pleading in Red Moon's eyes. And his English kept getting better with every new sentence he uttered. The man had a subtle, but unmistakable, ability to make his meanings clear and to impart a special importance to his words, no matter how simply spoken. It was obvious the Indian needed to recover his horse on his own, in his own way. Edward imagined it had something to do with pride or duty or some other such cultural dictate. He decided not to push or countermand it.

"Very well," he said, sitting back down under the shade of the rocks above them. "I will wait here for you."

Red Moon's features relaxed. A small grin, then: "Not much time. I...promise. Please – do not follow."

With those words, he turned and walked off in the direction they had already traversed, heading back towards the decline into the Judith River basin. Edward had no idea what he had in mind, but he found himself relishing the opportunity to relax his own bones. For an unarticulated reason, he felt secure. Perhaps because he knew there was a friendly Indian in the vicinity. Whatever the reason, he stretched out under the shade of the rock shelf, inclined his head to rest on his shoulder and extended arm. Not the most accommodating conditions for sleep, but he was soon dozing off into a well-anticipated nap.

5

"ALL GOOD NOW."

The words were spoken softly, pulling him from sleep as though by a gentle touch. For an instant, Edward experienced that odd disorientation of not knowing or remembering where he was. Then as his vision cleared, he looked up to see Red Moon standing close by. Behind him, still as a statue, a black mare with a shiny coat stood as if at guard.

"You found her!" Edward sat up, adjusted his hat over his brow.

"Yes. Not far."

Reaching into his trouser pocket, Edward glanced at his pocket watch. "How long was I asleep?"

"Long enough to find horse."

Edward chuckled at that, then stood up. "It's well past noon. I'd better be heading back to camp and get something to eat. Hungry?"

"Some."

"You are welcome to join me. My cook always has enough to go around."

"Where your camp?"

"East. Where the sun rises. A short ride on a slow horse."

"Edward Cope, you are a good man. Not like some others."

"You mean like other white men, don't you?"

"Yes, but good and bad men of all colors. I not mean to say wrong of your people."

Edward moved to his tethered horse. "No harm taken. Ready?"

Climbing upon the black mare, Red Moon nodded. "I follow."

They rode on for several minutes in silence, then the medicine man spoke: "Where you come from, Edward Cope? You not like many white men I see out here."

"I come from a place far, far away from here. So far that it takes three or four days by train to get out this way. A big place. Many big buildings, wide streets of brick, and many thousands of people and wagons. It is called Philadelphia. It is called a city."

"I know city called 'Dodge.' It like that?"

Edward grinned. "Not exactly. They might call Dodge a 'city,' but it is not. Two or three streets, maybe. Philadelphia has many *hundreds* of streets."

"Hmm, yes…that speak of very big place. If you live there, why you come here, Edward? Where nothing but rocks."

"Ah, but it is what is *in* the rocks! That is why I come here."

"In rocks?" Red Moon looked at him with a bemused expression.

Edward paused. How to explain to this man about his work? His passion. How to describe the fossils themselves, what they were, what they represented…or worse, how to explain what the fossils indicated about the age of the earth and the great and terrible creatures that once stalked and roamed these lands? Before meeting Red Moon, he would never have considered explaining the concept of paleontology to an Indian; but he knew for certain the man riding next to him was a very bright and very deep individual. Certainly not the "savage" stereotype the majority of the civilized world bandied about with utter disdain, if not outright contempt.

"Let me try to explain what I mean."

"You tell. I listen."

"Believe it or not, there are the bones of animals buried within some of the rocks and lands all around us. Animals that lived a long time ago. Many of them of great size. The bones of these creatures have lain under the earth for a long, long time. Longer than any of us could ever imagine. They tell of a world so different from this one, the one we live in. And the most surprising thing about them is that no one knew they existed! Until quite recently. My…my job is to find the bones and dig them up. Then take them back to Philadelphia where they can be studied."

Red Moon nodded in understanding, but also something else. "Yes, we call them *baakaxpi.*"

His words brought Edward up short. So shocked that he tugged on his horse's reins and brought the steed to a halt. "What did you say?! You know of these bones?"

Red Moon halted his horse as well, turned to regard Edward. "The bones, yes. But I also know the animals, the *baakaxpi*. There are many kinds. Some small and some very, very big."

Edward broke into a wide smile. The idea that the Indian knew of fossils advanced his pulse. Could they possibly help him in his endless quests? "This is absolutely astonishing! Do you know where I might find some of their bones? Have you ever seen them sticking out of the earth?"

"I have seen bones. Not in ground like you say. But *on* ground."

Edward tugged at his mustache nervously. It was a habit he'd developed whenever something excited him. "Oh my God, this is quite amazing. Can you take me to them? Show them to me?"

Red Moon shook his head. "No. This not easy thing."

"Why not? Is it far from here?"

"You could say that."

"I don't follow you. Why can't I see them?" His mouth was getting dry. He reached for the canteen from his saddlebag, opened it and sipped water. He offered it to his companion who shook his head, then spoke.

"They not here."

"Wait, wait! You just said you've seen them *on the ground.*"

"Yes, but in a…different…time. Not…*this* time."

"Damn it, man, you are not making good sense! What are you talking about?"

"Let us ride on, Edward Cope. I try to make you know what I say. What I do."

Edward agreed that they should keep moving. Best to get back to camp, get some sustenance. "All right, let's get going then. As you say, 'You talk, I listen.'"

As they began a steady pace along the edge of the river basin, Red Moon began his story with a question. "You know the word *skinwalker?*"

Edward shook his head. "No. Never heard of it. Can't say it sounds all that pleasant though."

Red Moon uttered a short half chuckle. "That very true. In some tribes, there are people who can…change themselves."

"Change? In what way?"

"The way they look. They be bird or wolf or bear. Anything they want."

"You mean they can disguise themselves to *look like* an animal?"

"No, Edward Cope. I mean they *be* the animal."

"What? That's…that's preposterous!"

"Not heard that word. But it sound not good."

Edward finally knew what the Indian was talking about. Legends abounded through many cultures regarding shapeshifters and were-creatures. And of course it was all a bunch of mythologies intended to frighten children or keep ignorant masses in check. But he did not wish to offend Red Moon by admonishing him.

"I'm sorry," said Edward. "I…I am just so surprised, is all. I have never encountered anyone who could do such a thing. Why do you bring it up? Are you trying to suggest that *you* are a 'skinwalker'?"

"No, not me. But I believe there be people like that. I tell you there be many things in the world. Many things we not know."

"You are talking about the true mysteries of existence. Yes, I think of them often." Edward considered his words carefully. He was a man of empiricism first and foremost, and as such, did not cotton to tales of the "unexplained" unless there was something grounding the phenomenon in a possible explanation via known science. That said, he did *not* think all that often of the outré aspects of what we call *reality*. If Red Moon was the shaman he claimed to be, it was not surprising the Indian would be involved with such fringe notions as shape-changers. Edward decided it best to simply humor the man and his far-flung fantasies.

He paused in his mental ramblings to orient their position along the route back to camp. Acknowledging several landmarks, he guided his horse along a rising path through an arroyo. "We are close to camp." he said to Red Moon.

"Good. But…there is more to tell you."

Edward looked over at the Indian and nodded. "I am still listening."

"Did you ask how I find my horse? How I not want you with me?"

Edward found the question a bit odd. He was also becoming ever more impressed with the man's command of English. It was almost unsettling. In addition, he had no idea where Red Moon was directing their conversation. After a pause he addressed the Indian's question: "Actually, no. To be honest, I had not given it much thought. I simply imagined you were a good tracker."

"No matter. It is more than that."

"Very well. I am, as they say, all ears." Edward gave his reins a gentle snap and his horse ambled forward at a slow but steady gate.

"I found my horse by going to the time when she left me, when she jumped back from the snake and ran. I watched from that…that moment. And followed her to where she stood in the now."

Edward heard each and every word, but he still found himself uncomprehending what they actually meant. "I am so sorry. But, I do not understand."

"Edward Cope, listen to me: I am a *timewalker*."

6

FOR SOME REASON, ALTHOUGH he'd never heard the word before, its utterance reached some deep core within him. Like a gentle bolt of lightning (if there could be such a thing), he felt it strike and wake him to a new level of awareness. Again, he had to rein his horse to a stop so he could fully engage his companion. Red Moon did the same and now stared at him with large dark eyes while their mounts again took respite under the afternoon sun.

"And I suppose you will be telling me what that *is*…"

Red Moon nodded. "I must."

"I have no idea what a 'timewalker' might be, but my imagination staggers under the possibilities."

"The plants I seek help me create what you call 'potions.' When I drink them, I can see things few people see." Red Moon gestured with an expansive sweep of the sky and the landscape.

The Indian's words caused a brief shudder in Edward. He still did not know what the shaman could be meaning, but the suggestion was disturbing enough. "What kinds of things?"

"Best word I know you understand be a *door*…a way get from one place…or time…to another."

Edward worried his mustache, then spoke: "That does not seem possible. What do you mean, literally? That you can see, for want of better words, 'doors into the past'…and that you can actually walk *through* them?"

Red Moon nodded slowly. "Yes. I do that thing. It how I find my horse. Look through 'door'…see where she go after she run from snake."

"What you are telling is simply not…possible!"

"It be so." Red Moon pointed across the terrain of ravines and steep hills. "There are many, many doors, everywhere. Not for most men to ever see. Not for most to pass through."

Edward paused to mentally parse what he was hearing from the medicine man, the shaman, or whatever he actually was to his people. The notion of seeing through time, *going* through time, struck him as so outlandish, so *unthinkable*…and yet the Indian spoke of it with such a casual demeanor. As if it were nothing special. He'd made no dramatic effort to convince Edward of his abilities. Just a few matter-of-fact statements. He did not sound like a braggadocio or a boasting fool. Most curious and perplexing, all at once. He regarded the Indian astride his black mare, who appeared to be content to wait in silence for Edward's eventual reply.

"Red Moon, I hope you understand when I say I am having a hard time *believing* you. I do not mean I say you lie. Speak not true. I do not say this. But…" He paused, held his hands out, palms upward in a gesture of frustration.

"You need no believe. You will see for own eyes." Red Moon spoke softly, his intonation suggesting great wisdom and assuredness.

The words somehow chilled Edward, and he was not sure why. Was he that afraid of discovering that the precious and lofty science of his world was not the endpoint, the true summit of man's knowledge? He grappled with that thought, disturbing as it might be, and said: "Yes. Yes, I would like that very much."

Red Moon said nothing.

Taking that as a signal their conversation was, for the moment, at an end, Edward snapped his horse's reins and chucked his stirrups. Goaded into motion, the horse began to head forward. Red Moon's mare followed, and they worked their way back to the expedition's camp.

7

WHEN THIBODEAUX SAW EDWARD approach with an Indian in tow, he could not hide his surprise. "Professor, you are late for lunch! And you have brought such a guest?!"

"That I have."

"Is he our new guide?"

"No, Frenchy, this is Red Moon. He is a Crow, from a friendly tribe, but not a guide. And by the way, we *are* hungry." Edward dismounted and walked his roan to the edge of the camp where he hitched the horse to a wagon wheel. He motioned for his companion to do the same. Other than Thibodeaux, the camp was deserted, which was not unusual. George Sternberg would have his crews out working on the current fossil sites until an hour before dusk.

As the camp cook dished out bowls of jackrabbit stew, Edward casually related the details of his encounter with the Indian, leaving out the most recent revelations regarding Red Moon's special abilities. Still fresh in his mind, Edward continued to grapple with the reality of the shaman's claims. Being ever the empiricist, he was going to have to see the evidence firsthand. In science, there remained little room for something so ephemeral as *belief*. For Edward, there was only fact. Something that had no need of man's faith.

Sitting across from Red Moon, Edward regarded the Indian with a strange mixture of fear and admiration. Fear that his claims may actually be true, and admiration of his seeming ease and comfort associating with an eccentric "pale face" like himself.

"How you like the stew?" he said, grinning.

Red Moon tapped the rim of his tin pan where the remnants of his meal awaited a final spoonful. "Good. Your man make good rabbit. Thank you."

"Happy to be able to provide it. My people call this sort of thing 'breaking bread.' It is a…a symbol. A sign of peace between men."

Red Moon nodded, placed his tin plate on the ground by his moccasined feet. "Yes. My people do same."

Edward nodded and signaled for Thibodeaux to collect their plates and utensils, then stood to face his dinner guest. "I suppose you know we need to talk a little more."

Red Moon stood as well. "Yes. I know we need talk."

"This way." Edward moved off toward the far end of the encampment where his heavy canvas tent had been pitched. Red Moon followed.

Arriving in his "private place," Edward gestured towards a campaign chair that faced the stone ring of a dead campfire. "Sit."

The Indian shook his head and sat upon the ground cross-legged as he pointed at the chair. "For you. I better like this."

"Okay," said Edward, taking a seat. "Now that our bellies are full, let's talk about…about what you said earlier. That I won't need to believe anything, because…I will be *seeing* it with my own peepers?"

Red Moon appeared puzzled. "*Peepers*. I not know that word."

Edward chuckled, ringed his thumbs and forefingers around his eyes. "Sorry. These. My eyes."

Red Moon nodded, grinned. His dark eyes, staring at Edward. "Oh, yes – eyes. But, yes. You see. True, Edward Cope."

"Well then, my next question should not surprise you. *When* shall we make this so?"

"I need return to my tribe. Need things…plants…to see. Then I come back for you."

Edward nodded. "A lot of men – my people – would hear those words and not believe you. That you would ever come back. Not me."

Red Moon got to his feet. His motions were graceful and fluid despite his years. His features were sharp and full of what the novelists called *character*, not just lines and wrinkles. "Edward Cope, I tell you before. You save me from coyotes. From die. My life now *your* life."

"I understand that." Edward moved closer to the shaman, who was inches shorter, but not looking at all frail for his age. "But we can be better than that. We can be friends, yes."

Red Moon grasped Edward's hand. "Yes. Friend better than...I do not have the word."

Edward smiled, shook Red Moon's hand forcefully. "*Obligation*. It means doing something but not really wanting to do. That is not what we have. What we want."

Red Moon's firm grip reciprocated Edward's as he spoke: "Yes. Friends."

Edward walked him to where the black mare waited to be unhitched from the wagon wheel, watched the Indian mount his horse. "For now, Edward Cope."

"Yes. You know where to find me." Edward jerked a thumb eastward. "I am always here when the sun is first in the sky. Then I ride off to look for signs of bones."

"I can help you with that." Red Moon touched his index finger to his forehead, then tapped his mare's flanks, turning her gently towards the basin trail.

Edward stood watching his new friend – an Indian, by God! – glide off into the twilight as his horse loped along at a leisurely gait. Spending time with Red Moon had been a strange but fascinating experience for Edward. There existed nothing in his wide range of encounters with hundreds of colleagues and thousands of students even remotely similar to his immersive hours with the shaman who claimed to be able to not only see through time, but *walk* through it.

Shaking his head as if to clear it of such an outlandish idea, Edward gathered up some tinder and kindling to make a campfire adequate to percolate a few tin cups of coffee. Caffeine remained one of his only real vices, and although the beans and grinds available in the Territories, when compared with the European and South American blends available in Philadelphia, proved mostly harsh and bitter, he still enjoyed several cups at the end of a long day.

He sat in his campaign chair as dusk overtook him and the camp, sipping with contentment and thoughts of Zeke's quest, the possible confirmation of a *compsagnathus* in North America, and of course a replay of the day's events and what they may bring in the future.

Within the hour, Sternberg led a bedraggled troop of students and several hired hands into the camp. To a man, they looked like all the starch had been beaten out of them by a high sun and lots of unyielding stone. Edward watched his primary assistant accept his supper offering from Frenchy, then head toward the campfire still warming a pot of strong coffee.

"Evening, Edward," he said, pulling up the other campaign chair, then placing his plate on his lap. "Did you enjoy an eventful day?

Edward lowered his cup, ran his fingers over one side of his mustache, and chuckled. "You might say that, my friend…"

Sternberg cocked his head like a quizzical dog. "I detect equal parts humor and weariness in those words. Do you have a story to tell?"

"That I do. I experienced one of those days unlike most which smack of the hum-drum – even out here in the wilds."

"Well, now you've really got me curious." Sternberg shoveled in some stew as he leaned forward in his seat. "I am all ears."

Edward spent the next half hour relating every detail of his encounter with Red Moon. On occasion, George interjected with a question or a request for a clarification, but in the main listened with attention most rapt. When Edward reached the point which involved his final conversations with the shaman – the ones which revealed his special ability to "timewalk" – he hesitated.

And George Sternberg picked up on it.

"What's wrong, Edward? You look suddenly flummoxed."

"No, not that. Just…indecisive, I wager."

"About what?" Sternberg reached into his vest, pulled out his corncob pipe and small pouch of tobacco. He began the ritual of carefully stuffing it before striking a match to its burnt-edged bowl.

"George, you know me to be a man of science, correct? A man not given to fanciful notions, to any such sort of tomfoolery or fabrications, right?"

Sternberg puffed like a steam locomotive, chuckled in between billowing clouds of smoke. "Without question. You are as down to earth as any man I know."

"Thank you. I...I guess, given what I am about to tell you, I needed to hear that."

"All right, you've certainly shown a heretofore unseen flare for drama, for a bit of suspense." Sternberg grinned with no small amount of slyness. "Are you fixing to tell me or *not?*"

Edward exhaled long and low. "I am not sure I should be sharing this last bit of information. I have no idea if Red Moon would approve of me telling this about him, but George, I swear I cannot keep it bottled up within me. It's too much for me to carry in solitude."

Sternberg peered at him through his pipe smoke. "Well, then you haven't much choice other than to unburden yourself."

Edward set down his tin cup on a rock by the edge of the embering fire, then sat with folded hands in his lap. He revealed the rest of Red Moon's tale as if he were a funeral director going through the prices of his list of services and products. He tried to not show anything to indicate he would, or would not, believe any of what the Indian had confessed to him. Just a matter of fact re-telling of what had been told to him. He tried to be as dispassionate as if he were delivering a scientific monograph to a group of academics.

When he finished, Sternberg said nothing at first, then: "I suppose the first thing I need ask is this: Do you believe him?"

"Although I've not known the Indian for very long, he does not strike me as the type to lie. There is a...a *noble* aspect to him. As the medicine man of his tribe, he takes that responsibility with all due seriousness."

"So you believe him."

Edward wagged his index finger. "Not exactly. Let's just say that I *want* to believe him."

Sternberg laughed. "Well of *course* you do! Damnation, so do I! Can you imagine what it could do for our expedition if it were true?"

"I'm not sure I can, actually. I need to see it for myself." Edward poured out the last of the coffee, now surely burned and bitter. "If Red Moon merely *tells* me what he is seeing when he goes into a trance (or whatever he does with his plant potions), that is no real proof that he is seeing anything at all."

"Precisely my thought as well," said Sternberg. His pipe extinguished, he tapped out the plug against the sole of his boot. "We can have no room for chicanery."

"I agree, but please, Charles…refrain from the word 'we' for the moment. I don't want the Indian to know I've told anyone of his claims. If there is any chance that would scare him off, I want to avoid it."

"Understood. I can keep my trap shut."

Edward nodded. "I know you can. That is why I felt I could tell you in the first place."

"When do you expect him to return?"

"Not certain. He said he needed to acquire the proper makings for his potions back at Crow Nation's present settlement. He could show up tomorrow, or perhaps the next day, or—"

"Or never." Sternberg huffed once.

"Yes, there is certainly that possibility, but don't forget, he believes I saved his life, and according to his people, his life now belongs to me. He is now beholden to me. I am like his…his *master* now."

Sternberg stood up, arched his back. "That is quite a responsibility. A man of lesser qualities could take quite advantage of Red Moon."

"I can only imagine what that weasel Marsh would do in a similar situation."

"Marsh! Just the mention of his name *disgusts* me…"

Edward shook his head slowly. "Did I tell you what he told the station master at Cheyenne, the last he was through there?"

"No, what did he say?"

"He said that I had a wife dying of consumption and I had abandoned her to take up with a saloon girl from Deadwood. He said it would be wise for people in Cheyenne to refuse to do business with the likes of a scoundrel such as me."

"Dastardly – the only word for him. But it's not the first time he's tried to slander you or undermine your efforts."

Edward allowed himself a small smile. "No. Just the most recent."

Sternberg stretched out his back again. "Well, enough about him. I'm going to do a bit of reading before turning in. Good night, Edward."

He bid his colleague the same, then returned to his seat. Tilting back a few degrees, he stared at the oncoming night sky where so many stars burned and sparkled. No one back east ever saw such awe-inspiring sights as the star fields above the Territories, and there were few words to describe them in their true magnificence.

He sat there staring for a few minutes before retiring to his tent. He was growing tired, but sleep did not come easy to him. While his body craved rest, his mind continued to churn with weird imaginings of what he might witness if Red Moon had spoken the truth.

8

THE NEXT DAY CAME and went, with no sign of Red Moon.

Edward had spent his time exploring the regions west of their current digs, sketching out a variety of possible sites in his notebook and tagging them with margin scribbles about landmarks to find them again. It was part of his normal routine, which included short visits to the digs where Sternberg's crews of students and range-hands continued to separate bone from rock – an often tedious process. The larger bones now suggested some type of hadrosaur. The smaller, more delicate ones seemed ready to yield enough of themselves to allow a definite identification.

After everyone returned to camp and had their fill at Frenchy's wagon, Sternberg repeated his evening ritual of sitting with Edward around the dying coals of his fire.

As nightfall enveloped the two men, George gave him a detailed report of that day's digging. Two of the rowdies had gotten into a scrap, and the rest of the team had to separate them. George issued warnings to both that such behavior couldn't be tolerated if they wanted to continue to be paid handsomely. He also relayed the news that the fossils of the smaller creature were just about freed and if it was not the same species of *Compsognathus* found in Germany, then it was a close cousin indeed.

Edward smiled at this. "That is excellent news! An opportunity perhaps to name a new species is always a pleasure."

"Of course," said George, pausing to exhale slowly. "Now a bit of, shall we say, *less* happy news…"

He went on to describe how the fossilized bones of the larger animal were not coming out of the ground very easily, and as a result, there had been quite a few fractures and splits. This was not uncommon in certain kinds of limestone deposits. Soon they would have to decide if their efforts were worth the trouble.

Then there came a pause in their conversation, which felt to Edward to be edging close to something of an awkward silence. Sternberg pretended to be fussing with his pipe, scraping out the bowl with his Barlow pocketknife.

Edward spoke first. "I know what you're thinking. I've been *had*, right? Had by a clever savage who is at this very moment probably laughing up his buckskin sleeve."

"Now, now. I've said no such thing. Although the notion *has* crossed my mind." George smiled.

"Mine as well. As much I hate to admit it. Especially since I meant what I said about the Indian. There is something about him, something…noble. I cannot let myself believe him capable of trickery or foolishness."

"I hope you're right, Edward. Hell, I *pray* you are!" George chuckled softly.

"And then there is Zeke," said Edward. "It's two days he's been gone. If all transpired as planned at the depot, he should be back tomorrow with a new guide."

"Well, we haven't need of a guide for the moment anyway, what with our dig keeping us put for at least a few more days."

"You're right. The timing is in our favor."

Another brief pause in their exchange, then Sternberg stood and glanced upward at the insane splash of stars. "What magic do we touch, Edward? To unlock the mysteries of the forever time, and labor under the unknowable above our heads…!"

Edward remained seated, but smiled as he smoothed his mustache. "I never knew you to be such the poet."

"I'm not, but for the fraud of my posturing. It's just that sometimes, the enormity of what we attempt hits me aside my head. Think of it, Edward! Fifty years ago, other than a select few like Buckland and Owen, not a soul upon this earth had any inkling of the giant majestic beasts who strode the earth so long before us!"

Edward nodded. "So true. The ignorance of science in that regard is both an embarrassment and a revelation. And even today, in the age of enlightenment, there are so many who believe the earth was formed a scant four thousand years ago."

"Fools! There will always be fools among us." Sternberg chuckled, then tilted his head as he raised one eyebrow. "Tell me, Edward, do you have anything stronger than coffee at this hour. Our dissertations have inspired in me a need for whiskey."

So unexpected was Sternberg's remark, that Edward laughed out loud. "George, I suspect you already knew I have some of Kentucky's finest."

Sternberg watched him enter his tent, the re-emerge with a bottle of Evan Williams bourbon. He popped the cap and poured a few drams of the precious amber into each of their tin coffee cups. "This is the last of it till we reach Cheyenne," said Edward. Was he such a bad person to not wish to share his private stash of good bourbon with anyone? Even an esteemed colleague such as Sternberg?

Banishing such thoughts, he raised his cup in a toast. "Cheers! May tomorrow bring us all we need!"

"I'll drink to that." Sternberg knocked back his portion with a flourish, almost tipping his bowler off his head.

Edward chose to sip and savor his own ration. He never understood the cowboy saloon practice of throwing a good whiskey down your throat in an instant.

He watched Sternberg stand and adjust his hat, then place his empty cup on the arm of his campaign chair. "Thank you, Edward. That was a fitting cap to the night. I look forward to the events of the day to come."

"As do I," said Edward, not getting up from his seat. "Good night, George."

He watched his friend and colleague walk his bow-legged walk back to his own tent, then chanced another small sip of his bourbon. It burned with its expected oaky sweetness, and he craned his neck up to regard the starry wonder of the endless firmament. As was his fashion, this was his way of unwinding from a long day. It usually proved the balm he needed to relax and accept the day just afforded him. But tonight, despite his bourbon and the stars, he felt agitated and even a bit angered – something he tried to avoid in accord with his Quaker upbringing.

He had fully expected to see Red Moon this day, and his failure to appear had been an embarrassment to Edward – even if only in the eyes of Sternberg. None of the other members of the expedition knew even a whit of what the shaman had promised. Tomorrow was most likely a lynchpin day for him. If the Indian did not show up, and Zeke *did* with a new guide anxious to lead them further west into the Territories, then Edward had a fairly significant decision to make. It was certainly possible Sternberg's dig would be at an end by mid-day. Did they break camp and move west and south of the Crow Nation, thereby cutting any ties with Red Moon and his outlandish claim to help Edward uncover a veritable trove of heretofore unknown fossils? Or did he wait one more day?

Such were the questions plaguing him as he retired to his tent and his bedroll. They capered and gibbered through his thoughts till sleep finally overtook him.

9

DAWN SEEPED INTO THE open folds of his tent flap as Edward opened his eyes to the faint but insistent light. He usually awoke just before sunrise, acceding to some somatic alarm clock deep within him, but this morning he stirred to consciousness feeling slow and fuzzy. Now why should that be? Was he not wishing to face whatever the day might have in store for him? That wasn't his usual demeanor. His dedicated passion for truth and accomplishment never allowed him to shirk from any kind of duty, task, or expectation. So what was dragging him down this morning? What sort of anchor had been tossed behind his wake?

Sitting up, wiping wispy crusts of sleep from his eyes, Edward knew what belabored him. Red Moon.

Did events of the day dictate him abandoning the Crow shaman? He was not prone to anxiety, thus the situation demanding his attention and decision presented him with an unfamiliar dilemma. Usually, his razor-sharp decisiveness left him feeling confident and often cocksure. But he felt none of that in the earliest moments of the new day.

After his routine morning ministrations and a breakfast of biscuits, hardtack, and coffee, Edward prepared for the day by checking his notes and his maps. If nothing else, he would continue his scouting expeditions into the expanded Territories for possible fossil deposits. The month of June was just about behind them, which meant another six to eight weeks of optimum weather and time to maximize their fossil hunting. He was determined to make the best of it – with or without Red Moon. As he gathered the items he would need for a day of careful searching, he heard Thibodeaux calling for him.

He advanced on the chuck wagon to see the cook waving his arms excitedly.

"What's going on, Frenchy?"

"Riders approaching. From the southeast." The cook pointed in that direction where a tell-tale dust plume indicated the coming of horses along the arid plain.

"I see it," said Edward. He adjusted his hat tighter across his brow and walked to the opposite end of the camp as the riders approached.

Within minutes the encroaching intruders resolved themselves into the familiar figures of Zeke Hardesty and Harley Woodward – two roughnecks whom Edward needed to trust in the best and the worst of times. He watched them gallop towards camp, their horses' steady gait neither frantic nor relaxed. Standing with his hands on his hips, Edward awaited Zeke, who rode lead until he reined in his mount as he pulled up in front of the professor.

Zeke jumped down from his saddle in great agitation. "Doc! Doc! You all good here?!"

"Yes, of course. Why should we not be?"

"We headed out middle of last night. Figured it was safer to be out after dark." Zeke squinched up his eyes, rubbed them. "While we was at the depot, word came through about General Custer."

Edward knew the name from his conversations with U. S. Army personnel at various outposts. Custer had a reputation for being a brash risk-taker. "What word? What about him."

"Two days back or so, his 7th Cavalry got tore up bad. Lakota Sioux mostly, but some Cheyenne and Arapaho, we heared. Killed 270 soldiers, including Custer."

Edward paused to take this in. It sounded like a significant loss for the U. S. Cavalry, and he wondered what it implied for him and the safety of his expedition. "Where did this happen?"

Zeke removed his hat, smacked it upon his thigh, then raked his greasy dark hair with his hand, before reseating the Stetson. "Little Big Horn River. Southeast territory. Crazy Horse done it! Hear tell he's one helluva fighter."

"How far from us? Are *we* in jeopardy?"

Zeke shook his head. "I don't figure. The lieutenant at the depot said the Injuns will probably split up into smaller bands for a while. Scatter east and north to keep from being attacked by any forces we might send to retaliate."

Harley had dismounted and walked up to join Zeke, but said nothing.

"Do you think he's right?" said Edward.

"Dunno, but he sounded pretty confident."

"What about the guide? I must presume no luck on that front since I only see the two of you." Edward smoothed out the right strand of his mustache.

"Well, Doc... When word got out about Custer, the few Injun guides workin' at the depot lit out. Most folks figured they got spooked. Didn't want to be caught hangin' out with the white man in an attack, right?"

Edward nodded. "Makes sense. These developments may dictate a change of our plans. I'll consult with Sternberg."

"Okey-doke," said Zeke. "As long as we get paid, we're up for whatever you want."

Harley flashed his toothy tobacco-stained smile. "Yessir, Doc. You can count on us."

Edward regarded them as he paused for a moment. These types were only loyal to one thing: the U. S. Dollar. "Thank you, gentlemen. Go get some chow from Frenchy and rest your bones a spell."

As Edward turned to seek out Charles, Zeke spoke up. "Oh, wait – there *is* one more thing..."

"I am almost afraid to ask... What is it?"

"Well, while we were tryin' to be certain there weren't no guides to be had—"

"In the Black Hills Saloon!" said Harley.

Zeke cut his companion a heavy-browed look that Edward would have called almost murderous. Spending time in venues where liquor and gambling and loose women prevailed were hardly pursuits he was paying them to do. In truth, Edward did not care what his ruffians did every minute of their days. If they managed to complete their tasks, *that* proved most important to him. And the horrible massacre at Little Big Horn certainly absolved them of their inability to find a suitable guide.

And so he said nothing, just a simple hand gesture urging Zeke to continue.

"Well, yeah... We was in the saloon, talkin' to folks, tryin' to get a lead on any Injun who might be right fer us. Or maybe an ex-Army type lookin' for work. Like Henry Dawkins, if you recall... You know how that is, and that's when we saw him and he saw us."

"*Who* saw you?" Edward was just discovering that Zeke had an uncanny ability to make things as suspenseful as possible without any sense of how to create true drama.

"Black Dan McKay. He must have overheard some of our talkin's, or he had people at the depot that reported to him."

"Yeah," said Harley, no longer smiling. "He sidled right up to us at the bar and asked us, point blank, where *you* might be. All dressed in black and lookin' his usual self."

The mention of McKay gave Edward a galvanic start, as if he could feel a hitch in his heart. "What...what did you tell him?"

Harley grinned half-wise. "Well, that's when Zeke here pulled a fast one. He told Dan we been southeast near the border, near the Sioux uprising and the Little Big Horn battle...which we'd just heared of. And that we were fixin' to head east right quick like."

Edward inclined his head, focused his gaze on the two of them. "Did he believe you?"

Zeke shrugged. "Hard to say. McKay, he gots a face like a slab-a stone. Might tough to read. Did give us a nod and smile though. You can't miss that big gold tooth right off his front-un's. Kinda scary, it is."

Edward paused to consider this information. Then: "Do you have any idea why he might have been at the depot?"

"We thought the same thing. Asked around. He was buyin' supplies – food and materials. For Marsh, no doubt."

"So Marsh is close by... Damnation!" Edward mused out loud "In range of the Black Hills Depot or...at the least *somewhere* in the Montana Territories. Why couldn't he be in the Dakotas or Wyoming? Or even the Morrison Formation!?"

"Don't rightly know about all them places." Harley tugged at his gunbelt, adjusting it minutely to a better comfort level. He was not very bright, but he was something of an artist with his Colt .44. A good man to have around when the name of Black Dan McKay was mentioned. He tilted his head slyly and spoke: "We figures he wants to be where the best diney-sores are to be had…and that, Doc, is wherever *you* might find yerself."

Edward could not contain a brief chuckle. Despite the roughneck's limited faculties, he just could be right about that. Especially if Red Moon lived up to his promises. "Do you think he may have followed you back here?"

Zeke shook his head. "Doubtful. 'Specially since we headed out in the middle of the night last night."

"Yes," said Edward. "That was certainly a wise tactical maneuver on your part."

"Huh?" said Harley.

"He means we done good." Zeke smiled. "C'mon…let's eat."

Harley nodded, led his horse to the hitching wheel of the big buck-wagon, then followed Zeke to Frenchy's smaller cook station.

Watching them depart, Edward wondered what all this new information portended for him and his group of fossil hunters. The one thing he never wanted on his conscience was any decision which led to catastrophe or disaster for any of the earnest paleontology students, or even the cowhands he'd recruited for the summer months. He truly believed himself in a quandary. Did he proceed as if it were "business as usual"? Or did he gather everyone together for one of those democratic sessions where the fate of this year's expedition might very well be decided? When Edward considered the amount of money already allocated and spent on his endeavor, he felt physically ill at the thought of stopping now at mid-stream – that point where going forward or backward would demand equal amounts of risk and funding and effort.

Edward acknowledged the season had already produced some wonderful, and perhaps even historic, new finds, but also the notion of – dare he even *think* it? – Red Moon giving him the gift of *seeing* where new fossils may lie in wait of his keen eye and tiny pick-axe.

More to think about, he mused, the type of dilemma which normally excited him, challenged him. Day to day, Edward loved that thing – whatever it may be – which presented him with an intellectual proposition to be determined, to be solved. And so he stood by the flaps of his open tent weighing his options. The morning sky still held a generous smear of color: magenta, orange, a touch of indigo. The day bloomed young and fresh, awaiting his decisions.

Edward knew he would want to share his ruminations with Charles Sternberg, but that lay in the imminent future. Word of Black Dan McKay was synonymous with any mention of Charles Othniel Marsh. Just thinking of *either* of the men left Edward in a foul sort. And oddly enough, Edward still sometimes wished things between he and Marsh had not deteriorated to their present state. A folly, to be sure.

He'd first met Marsh in, of all places, Hamburg, Germany, while the United States Civil War burned hot and bright. Ironically, both of their families had found it wise to ship their young scions off to Europe to escape being drafted into that horrific conflict. At the time of their meeting, Edward found the man to be fulsome and resolute in his desire to be an honorable man of science. And so, in their earliest professional years, Edward and Charles Marsh had become friends and colleagues. But then things gradually, inexorably, changed. Marsh acquired the backing of his uncle to land a sinecure at Yale's Peabody Museum and became the *de facto* curator of the museum's myriad exhibits, especially its bones of long-ago beasts. Without much qualification or validation, "Professor" Marsh became the final arbiter of how fossil remains would be displayed or, more importantly, how they would be assembled in the first place...*before* they would be displayed to the public.

More or less about the same time, Edward had uncovered the fossil remains of a great sea-beast which had roamed the Great Kansas Sea of the mid-Cretaceous. It was an *Elasmosaurus* – a plesiosaur skeleton exhibiting quite exquisite preservation. When Edward had the fossil bones shipped east for reconstruction, he supervised the initial work to create the exhibit of the plesiosaur. So excited had he been to provide the citizens of Pennsylvania with such a wonder, that he did not notice the error of a museum laborer, who had attached the skull of the plesiosaur on the tip of its tail instead of its neck vertebrae. A complete and total opposite of its accurate anatomical representation.

When Charles Othniel Marsh and Joseph Leidy visited Cope's exhibition presenting the beautifully intact skeleton of the sea-going monster, he immediately noticed the gross error in the skull placement. But instead of approaching Edward in private to point out the antipodal mistake, he made a very public spectacle by allowing Leidy to re-position the skull on the *opposite end* of the skeletal remains – the skull no longer wrongly attached to the end of the beast's tail, but upon its proper neck vertebrae. The reverberations within the scientific community regarding this event and subsequent issue made Edward look the fool. Were it not for the catalogue of previous accomplishments by him, he would have been ostracized from the paleontological community as a mountebank.

And the entire embarrassment could have been avoided, had Marsh been a compassionate gentleman rather than a cad.

Edward had never forgotten that moment when Marsh chose one-up-man's-ship over professional courtesy. From that point on, they were no longer friends or even colleagues – they were rivals at best, but more realistically *enemies.*

10

HE THANKED HEAVEN FOR having such a thoughtful and wise colleague like Charles Sternberg as part of his team. After relating everything Zeke had told him, Edward set out the options ahead for the expedition, then waited for Sternberg's assessment.

He removed his bowler, raked a hand through his hair, then reseated the hat. "Even though we've already gathered some fine specimens, it's still too early to pack in and head for Cheyenne, don't you think?"

"My thought all along," said Edward. "What we've spent would not justify such a thing. The university wouldn't be pleased to not get their money's worth."

Sternberg nodded. "Everything eventually comes down to money."

"So you vote for staying on?"

"Of course. I think we move gradually, but inexorably west – away from the Sioux and the warpath tribes. But what that Army officer told Zeke makes sense. Most likely the culprits will split up into smaller groups to avoid discovery and punishment. We'll probably be safe enough."

"As safe as we ever are out in these parts." Edward grinned. "Then it's settled – business as usual."

Sternberg arose from his seat, checked his pocket watch. "Until something untoward makes us change our plan. I'd better get the crew on point. The day won't wait for us, and I'd like to get the rest of our bones free before it comes to an end."

"George, I appreciate you being my good and faithful sounding board. I know I am the leader of the band, but I don't think I could do it without you."

"Sure you could." Sternberg grinned. "Don't kid yourself. See you this evening."

And with that, he turned and walked off toward the group of students' tents along the edge of a shallow arroyo. Edward watched him go for a few scant seconds, then gathered up his daily gear and headed for his tethered roan. He could feel the heat of the morning dancing upon the back of his neck and he welcomed another summer day in Montana Territory.

11

AN HOUR LATER, HE'D finished sketching out possible sites beyond the box canyon of the previous few days' searches. As he paused for a judicious few sips of spring water from his canteen, he heard a familiar voice call out to him.

"Edward Cope!"

Reining his horse towards the direction of the sound, he regarded Red Moon astride his black mare in a posture that could be termed *regal*. With back straight and shoulders back, the Indian did not appear to be half the age Edward knew he must be. "Hello, my friend!" he called as he urged his horse into a gentle approach. "I have been wondering when I would see you again."

Red Moon nodded. "I rest some. Help my people some. Prepare for return to you. I here now."

Smiling, Edward extended his hand as his horse sidled alongside the mare. Red Moon took his hand in friendship. "Yes, you are. Yes, you certainly are. I *knew* I would see you again."

Red Moon nodded. "Are you ready, Edward Cope? Are you ready to be a *timewalker*?"

As Edward released his grip, the Indian's words penetrated him as if arrows. He felt a kind of shock as the possible reality of what may now come stirred in him. The moment had come, had it not? When he would know if he was dealing with the stuff of legends and superstitions…or the unimagined power that capered beyond the veil of known science.

"Why yes, of course I am." He listened to the slight tremble in his voice; was that an indicator of his fear? In a sense, he hoped it was indeed.

If his journey would take him to a time so promised, then fear would be a healthy emotion to employ.

"Good. We now get ready. Go to small cave this way." Red Moon pointed in a westerly direction and touched his mare's flanks to get her moving. Edward followed as they paused now and then to gather tinder and sticks for a fire. Perhaps fifteen minutes passed until they reached the dark, cool entrance to a hollowing in the steep slope of a limestone formation.

Once inside, Red Moon sat cross-legged and quickly created a small fire encircled by stray stones and rocks. As the flames licked, he opened a sack made of sewn animal hide and from its depths produced a variety of dried plants, leaves, and what might have been strings of jerky from an unknown beast. He also removed several small bags that looked like the talismans some Indians wore around their necks. The last thing to emerge from the sack was a carved wooden bowl, into which Red Moon began to place the crumbled pinchings of the desiccated leaves as well as the powdery contents of the talisman bags.

Edward watched all the preparations in silence, fascinated by the precise, almost ritualistic manner in which Red Moon went about his business. But finally his curiosity could not be further contained. "Were you planning to tell me what any of that stuff is, the stuff going into the bowl?"

A long pause, and Edward started to assume the shaman would simply ignore his question, but then he spoke: "Things you not want to know. Dry bodies insects, animal dung. Not the most bad."

Just the mention of a few of the esoteric ingredients created a subtle churn in Edward's gut. Whatever else was getting ground into the central powder of the wooden bowl would eventually be a preparation intended to be ingested...by him. The mere *thought* of somehow swallowing Red Moon's concoction created such anathema within him, he had to stand up, bent beneath the low ceiling of the cave, and pace back and forth to alleviate his anxiety.

Insects? What kind exactly? Plant stems and leaves? Of what genus? *Dung?* Unthinkable!

"Soon," said Red Moon. He retrieved an Army issue canteen from his black mare's carry-belt and poured out a carefully measured amount of water into the bowl. Then he stirred the incongruous gruel for long minutes until it began to blend itself into a homogenous pabulum of a pale brown hue.

Watching over the shaman's shoulder from a cautious distance, Edward observed the multi-admixture finally achieve a kind of stasis of density and consistency. A thin but opaque liquid that most assuredly held a large number of particles in suspension, stirred under the constant circular movement of Red Moon's ministrations. Accompanying the ritual-like blending of the components, the shaman spoke an unending string of incantations in the lyrical, vowel-heavy language of the Crow.

Time, within the cool shadows of the cave, stretched to the point of meaninglessness, and Edward had no idea how long he'd hunched beneath its embrace. Watching the careful actions of Red Moon had an almost mesmerizing effect on him. He felt totally at ease, ready for whatever came next in his quest for truth. When he heard his name voiced, it was as if the syllables drifted across a vast and untrammeled gulf.

"Edward Cope…?"

"Yes," he said, hearing his own voice and marveling at its timbre. Was that *him* speaking? Indeed, it was.

"We are ready. For first walk."

"Yes, I am ready." His voice had acquired a soft, compliant tone.

Red Moon nodded slowly with implied solemnity, then, holding the wooden bowl in both hands, he raised it to his lips and quaffed half its muddy contents in several labored gulps. When finished, he turned to Edward and offered the bowl to him. "Drink. All."

Taking the bowl in both hands, Edward stared at the murky liquid with trepidation. "I was afraid you would be saying that."

Red Moon remained stoical, his eyes beginning to acquire a faraway glassiness.

"Drink, Edward Cope."

Screwing up his determination, Edward moved the bowl to his mouth, opened wide, and poured the libation liberally, filling his cheeks as he attempted to take in the entire serving in one quick swallow. He found the consistency to be like a thick gruel, and the taste was surprisingly bland, not the foul stew he'd expected. It went down without a hitch and he handed the empty bowl back to his shaman friend.

"Not bad," he said as he smoothed out both strands of his mustache, which held a few scant drops of the potion.

"Yes," said Red Moon, whose eyes had widened. He appeared to be staring off at something very far away. "Soon. You feel…not like you. You tell me when. I wait."

Sitting upon a large stone, legs splayed out as he leaned back against the inward curve of the cave wall, Edward was about to say he didn't feel a thing…when the *wave* crashed over him. One moment he was simply there as usual, casting a casual glance at his dusty cowboy boots, and then…everything in his peripheral vision, everything along the edges of his sight, began to shimmer and waver like objects in the distance during the mid-day burn of the desert. Then things elongated, as if he gazed down a long tube.

What in Sam Hill was happening? Whatever it was, it was happening *fast!*

He extended his arms out in front of him and they appeared impossibly long. Struggling to his feet, he wondered if he would be imbalanced, but he was not. "I feel…not myself," he said, as much to himself as to Red Moon.

The Indian approached him and took his hand, holding it lightly as if guiding a child. "We go now. Come."

Exiting the cave, Edward allowed himself to be guided out into a clear bright day – a day that dazzled and sparkled in ways he'd never experienced. Colors were more saturated, the edges of objects seemed somehow sharper, more cleanly delineated, contrasts between light and dark more obvious and easily discerned. Edward knew he saw the world in a manner never before imagined.

"Where are we going?" he said almost lazily. A sensation settled over him that was not lassitude as much as being totally comfortable with his present situation. No anxiety, no uncertainty, and definitely no panic. He trusted his companion. It was that simple.

Red Moon swept a hand across the landscape in front of them and for the first time Edward became aware of tiny black dots permeating *everything.* Then the black dots resolved into smaller spots of color. Reality had become a collection of an infinite number of specks of color and darkness that Edward could see up close and simultaneously far away.

"You see them," said Red Moon.

"Oh yes. Beautiful. Amazing." Edward knew exactly to what the Indian referred.

"Each one can open. Like window. Like door. We go in now."

A large part of Edward's awareness found this concept perfectly sensible, but a snippet of empirical wariness balked at the suggestion. "Into one of those…those *dots?* How in the Lord's name—?"

Before he could finish the question, Red Moon reached out and *touched* one of the dots with his index finger. Then he grabbed Edward by his arm, tugging him forward as one of the specks of color expanded to accommodate them, so much so they were able to actually *pass through* it…

…into another world.

The first thing he noticed was how *green* everything had become. Not merely green, but every hue and saturation of the most verdant landscape ever seen. The lush flora embraced them in soft shadows as they advanced upon a soft and loamy earth. It felt spongy beneath his boots. The air sizzled with the buzz of insects, punctuated by the erratic cries and honks of beasts, some of which sounded very close indeed. Ahead, he could see two stands of palm-like cycads opening to reveal the shoreline of a lake, their thick boles and trunks like unstaved barrels, accented by light brown cones. All around them giant tree ferns exploded with deep green fronds. It was more forest than jungle and never before seen by men of science. Large, black-limbed conifers grew here along with sparsely needled evergreens – primitive pines and spruces, tall proto-firs and cedars. Thick cypresses seemed to reach out like tentacled creatures, and unbranching hemlocks soared black and pencil-thin.

The scents of the place and time assaulted him, so strong and pungent, so alien. He had stopped, standing stock-still as he felt the total *strangeness* of this distant time seep into him like damp, evil fog. Red Moon, who had been several paces ahead, turned and reached out to him, tapping his arm.

"We need to keep moving, Edward Cope…"

"Sorry, I…I'm feeling a bit overwhelmed by all of it. It's *nothing* like Montana! I mean, in my mind, I knew the earth had been like this, but to actually see it! *Feel it!* I…don't know how to explain what I am feeling."

Red Moon looked at him with understanding in his eyes. "I too feel this way when first I walk in time. In some ways, feeling never go away. But please, we must move away from this place; too close to water. Everything come here to drink."

Edward considered this and it certainly made sense, but he wondered why the need for caution. "Yes, but the creatures, they cannot see us, can they?"

Hearing those words, Red Moon moved close and spoke with some urgency. "Edward Cope! Yes! They see us because we really *here*. We go away from here. *Now.*"

As the shaman's words reached him, and their meaning took hold in his mind, he felt a surge of sheer panic seize him. *Could it be?!* Why had he assumed they were just *peering* into this piece of time? He had to be sure he understood. "You mean— You mean we are actually *here*? Not just watching this place, this time, but we have somehow *entered into* it?"

Touching Edward's shoulder with a firm grip, Red Moon began guiding him through the lush vegetation, away from the watering hole, even though there existed no real trails or paths. "You not see through time, you *walk* through it. We are time*walkers*, Edward Cope. You. Here."

The words anchored him to that precise moment, and as he processed the dichotomy of what his mind knew was possible and *not* possible, he had no choice but to accept Red Moon's words as a simple truth. By whatever magic or science, they had stepped into time itself.

With every step, the reality of the earth so many tens of millions of years ago cascaded over him. A strange and wondrous place, teeming with an admixture of fragrances that spoke of both plant and animal. One of his initial observations: the sheer *density* of life in this time, defined by the endless cacophony of sounds, scents, and colors. Insects thrummed and darted everywhere as tiny creatures skittered and juked across his path with amazing frequency while the very ground trembled slightly from the far-off footfalls of something impossibly large.

Reaching out, he touched the shoulder of Red Moon, who led the way through the vegetation. "Without sounding the fool, I have to ask: Do you come here often?"

"Oft enough. I am, how to say…? In awe of this time of life. And also very much fear." The Indian did not look back as he spoke, but remained vigilant as they moved farther away from the water source.

"I can certainly understand that," said Edward. He grew increasingly aware of the humidity and the high temperatures. The earth had clearly been a much warmer place and he marveled at the contrast between the climes of the Montana of his era and this one.

A loud bellowing cry echoed through the dense jungle, so stark, so bold, it caused both men to stop mid-stride. "My God," said Edward. "What was *that*?"

"Something hungry," said Red Moon.

The raucous sound rolled over them again. Then something else screamed. A piercing, awful cry that was suddenly throttled.

Edward felt his innards churn and begin to drop deeper into his gut. He knew Red Moon was correct, but that sound also suggested an animal arrogance that said it didn't care if any other creature was now aware of its proximity or position. He pushed forward, following his guide, but he fought an ever-growing anxiety that could easily escalate to fear, or worse: panic. At that moment he became overwhelmed by an overriding sense of *not belonging here*. He was an intruder in this place, this *time*. To say the notion made him uncomfortable touched upon absurdity; he loathed the sensation, and felt utterly powerless to do anything about it.

The hungry roar pierced the primordial forest again, although sounding more distant than before. The suggestion of that eased his mind, even if only a smidgen. Every so often a thought shot through him – he knew he would never look upon the dry, dusty fossilized bones of a dinosaur again without thinking of where the beast had once lived and, eventually, expired.

In his peripheral vision, he caught movement overhead and glanced up just in time to see a reddish-brown pterosaur glide past them as it homed in on the water they had first seen. Barely skimming the tops of the tallest trees, its wingspan easily topped twenty feet. Incredible.

Scarcely had they moved another twenty feet or so when Edward heard sounds which suggested something moving through the woods at a deliberate pace. Red Moon, equally aware, signaled for them to pause, to look for whatever approached. He gestured for them to crouch down, and

Edward did so, but they did not need to wait long before seeing what lumbered near their position. Catching glimpses of a small herd of animals moving through a scattering of conifers, Edward recognized what he imagined to be some sort of duckbill herbivores. Standing perhaps twelve feet, they waddled on their hind legs toward the water. Edward smiled for the first time in this terrible era as he realized that many paleontologists' depictions of dinosaurs could differ quite a bit from their true forms. Drawings of hadrosaurs imagined them to be sleek and lean, perhaps semi-amphibious, but these duckbills looked pot-bellied and bottom-heavy. Their throats hung down from their jaws in loose folds of dewlap. Their movements were slow and deliberate, and he could not help notice the hadrosaurs required a significant time to properly right themselves on their hind legs after dropping down to drink.

As he contemplated all of this and planned to enter what he witnessed in his sketchbook, a sudden flash of motion and color burst from the vegetation to the right of the hadrosaur. Startling him and Red Moon, Edward heard a furious crackle and rustle of foliage from the forest's edge to his left. A tan and red blur of movement broke from the shaded tree-barrier. Something large and quick and half-again in height of the lumbering hadrosaur exploded from the heavy stand of trees. So unexpected, so shocking in its speed, a bipedal carnivore seemed to appear out of nowhere.

The sudden attack literally froze him mid-stride. *What was this thing?!* Despite the surging beat of his heart, he forced himself to focus on the terrifying scene. A bipedal carnivore had brazenly appeared from the primordial forest in an instant – just enough time for Edward to observe two things: the beast's bright red and tan colors, and spiky *feathers* along the sagittal crest of the predator's head.

Could such things be?

And then another thought struck him, tinged with bitter irony: he knew this monstrous creature. He'd originally discovered this dinosaur and had given it the name *Laelaps* in the professional journals, but he had been in error. None other than Charles Othniel Marsh was the first to chastise him for his error of nomenclature: the genus name "*Laelaps*" already belonged to an insect, a mite. Cope had been forced to accede to the renaming of the fossil remains by Marsh, who proclaimed that the bipedal predator be known as *Dryptosaurus*.

And now it capered before him; of all the possible beasts to encounter, why did it have to be *this* one? Standing twelve feet high and at least twenty in length, the beast ran on its hind legs in a forward lean, using its long, straight tail as a counterbalance – unlike the stiff upright stance imagined by many of Edward's colleagues. They had been very wrong indeed. Its smaller forelimbs extended in talon-like claws as if to attach upon its victim like grappling hooks.

Its prey, the dull brown waddling duckbill who had been the leader of the herd, sensed danger and tried to accelerate its gait, but the attacker lunged forward with an impossible burst of speed and pounced upon its back. For an instant the two creatures hung motionless as though captured on a photographic plate, balanced, not toppling, the mud brown hide of the prey in sharp contrast to the bold colors of the attacker. Then the *Dryptosaurus* slashed with its heavily muscled right thigh and splayed hindclaw, tearing a gaping wound from the victim's spine to knee-joint. The hadrosaur fell forward, slapping into the swampy mud with a muffled thud. Edward winced as he heard the fallen beast emit a weak, bleating cry, as if a wounded baby bird. He watched as the *Dryptosaurus* went in for the kill. It stood partially upright, firmly pinning its hindclaws into the body of its prey. Then in a movement so quick Edward could barely follow, its great jaws opened, flashed a razor set of teeth, and snapped viciously into the hadrosaur's exposed flanks. Ripping and jerking its head from side to side savagely the carnivore worried the flesh of its prey until a great bloody flap was torn from its side, exposing a glistening rib cage. The *Dryptosaurus* raised its head, holding piece of meat between its sharp teeth, tossing it slightly, then snapped its jaws once more. The entire gobbet of flesh disappeared into its mouth, distending the carnivore's throat as it passed.

As though energized by the first taste of blood, the attacker jammed its open jaws into the torn belly of the hadrosaur, ravaging and tearing out another section of still-quivering flesh. The victim trembled feebly under the weight of its killer, but to no avail. Its life fluids ran rampant from the hideous violation of its flank. Edward stood stock-still as he watched the horrible tableau of a helpless creature being eaten alive until its small bird-like eyes finally slid shut.

While the carnage played out and the predator settled in to feed upon its kill, the remainder of the small duckbill herd rushed away from the scene as quickly as their lumbering gaits would allow. Edward watched them disperse through the swampy, heavy mud of the shoreline until they could wade through the shallows to the relative safety of an adjacent shoal. Such a wrenching scene, he felt as helpless as he was terrified.

"My God," he said in hushed tones to Red Moon. "I had no idea…"

The Indian nodded. "It is the way of this time."

"So fast… So…*brutal*."

"This your first time. We can go back. Come again when you…more…ready."

Edward considered Red Moon's thoughtful and insightful words. The sheer terror that had gripped him as he'd watched the attack and kill had only gradually subsided as they held their position while the *Dryptosaurus* continued to feed. He wondered if he would ever be more "ready."

"Yes. Thank you. I think you are right. We go back now."

Adjusting his headband with the trailing feathers, Red Moon's expression was one of understanding. A slight nod, then: "We can go. Follow me."

But before they could take even a single step back from the area, a new commotion stopped them. From the thick vegetation behind the feeding *Dryptosaurus* came another furious burst of color and movement.

"Look!" cried Edward. So shocked, he gave no thought to revealing their position. He felt Red Moon's grip upon his bicep as the Indian also watched in silent amazement.

What impressed Edward the most about this time and place was the *speed* of the hunters, the predators. So fast. So unimaginably fast. And just as that thought touched him, in an eyeblink *another* creature had emerged from the forest and hurled itself headlong into the hunched bulk of the feeding *Dryptosaurus* – the commencement of an insane battle. The intruder's hide was also tan and red, its spine and head crested with bright feathers – a second *Dryptosaurus*, bigger and taller than its predecessor by several feet.

"We need go," said Red Moon.

Edward heard his companion speaking, but he remained transfixed by the two dinosaurs as they began to battle over the fresh kill. The intruder's initial impact had knocked the feeder off the carcass and onto its back, and as the beast struggled to right itself, the larger animal lunged forward, jaws wide open, to sink rows of curved teeth deep into the exposed throat of the smaller dryptosaur. A hideous scream pierced the air as the attacker buried his snout into the wound, thrashing and tearing. Gouts of blood and flesh littered the thick mud that had already begun to suck and sink the ruined remains of the *hadrosaur*.

"Edward Cope, we go!"

"Yes…" Edward replied, but he remained standing in the green shadows, unable to turn away from the incredible scene unfolding before him. The smaller dinosaur, even though mortally stricken and rolled over onto its back, kicked out with its muscled hind legs and raked across the almost-white underbelly of its attacker. Three deep slashes, like parted lips, burst forth with a bright red flood, causing the larger dryptosaur to give up the fight and leap off into shallows. At the same time, its victim flailed weakly at its ravaged throat with its small forelimbs. Edward watched as its motions became more erratic, then less controlled, as its life blood continued to spill forth from its gaping neck wound. The creature's jaws opened wide and it emitted one final, piercing scream before locking into a final rictus of death.

Ignoring this, the victorious predator shambled from the water through the mud, driven to scavenge whatever might be left of the hadrosaur. Scarlet still seeped from its belly, but the need to feed remained primal. Edward had never imagined such a totally savage and terrible world as this one. Even the air carried a heavy, humid, metallic scent of blood.

A tugging at his sleeve brought him back to himself, and he looked over at Red Moon, who indicated the direction they needed to go with a subtle tilt of his head. Edward followed without a word, his thoughts still a-jumble with what he had witnessed in this hellish place, this hellish time. Behind them, the air filled with new sounds: a furious, escalating buzz of giant insects and the caw-like screams of lower-level scavengers approaching the still-warm carrion flesh to be consumed. It would be easy to lose one's grip, to surrender to the horrors. Edward needed to be *away*. Now.

"Near. Soon." Red Moon's voice anchored him to a more rational state.

"Please, get me out of here." Edward heard his own voice and wondered who was speaking, almost laughed out loud when he realized it was himself. He knew he was stumbling forward through the thick, alien vegetation, but he had trouble focusing on any details of his surroundings, as if some kind of mental fog sought to distort his vision.

"Take my hand," said Red Moon. "We go."

Vaguely aware of his companion's grip, Edward stepped forward with the faith of a true believer. With a momentary ringing in his ears, he sensed a blue-white halo envelope them for an instant, and then...

...the dry, barren landscape of the Territory stretched out before them. Like turning the page in some immense book or clamping out the wick on a great lantern, they had returned in an instant from their travels through hell. Relief washed over him, and Edward sank to his knees as much in fatigue as in thankfulness. They were safely away from that world of monsters.

"Oh my God, Red Moon... Thank you! You have saved me!"

"Yes. We are safe now."

Moving to a small nearby boulder, Edward seated himself, produced a bandanna from his jacket, and mopped his sweaty face. "I...I had no idea! And you say you have traversed that place – that time – before?!"

Red Moon grinned. "Many times, Edward Cope."

The very idea of going back, of "timewalking" again, made him giddy and unmoored.

"How? Why?"

"Same reason dog licks his stick... Because he can."

Edward laughed long and hard. The tension and fear slipped free of him. "You know, even though I just experienced it, and I *know* it really happened, I am having trouble believing it."

Red Moon nodded. "Yes. Same for me. Many years ago. Many first times in our lives...same thing."

Looking at his companion, Edward appreciated his wisdom and understanding. But how could he be so calm, so at ease with what they'd just witnessed? He asked him as much and the Indian just shrugged and said: "All times, all places have things to...to scare us."

Edward nodded, adjusted his hat more squarely. "I suppose you are correct, but may I confess to you?"

"What is 'confess'?"

Edward grinned. "To tell a truth."

"Oh, yes. I see."

"After seeing and *being* there, I do not think I want to ever go back."

For what seemed like a *long* time, Red Moon sat motionless, without expression, as if Edward had not spoken to him. Then: "As you wish. But there something we should look for first."

"And what is that?"

Red Moon pointed to a slab of rock that canted upward into the hillside behind them. "Better I show. This way."

He followed his companion up the hillside maybe thirty yards, until Red Moon dropped to his knees, began brushing away the topsoil from an area where a jagged edge of sandstone emerged. Then he picked up a hand-sized rock and began to chip away at the edge. Edward knew immediately what he was attempting: to uncover a fossil!

"Look... Here." Red Moon pointed to something locked within the sandstone. "You get pick and brush."

Hunching down, Edward peered into the dirt and fractured stone to see the smooth almost straight leading edge of an object that could only be a length of exposed bone. He could actually feel his pulse jump. How could this shaman have known where to find this?

He asked him directly and for an instant Red Moon stared off into space with little expression, before pointing to the side of his head. "I do not know how. I just...*know.*"

"It's unbelievable! I will have to get Sternberg's team over here first thing in the morning." Edward rubbed his hands together in nervous anticipation. "Red Moon, in just one day, you have caused in me such a range of feelings, I feel both exhausted and energized. You are like a miracle!"

Red Moon could only shrug.

Chucking him lightly on the arm, Edward smiled. "Let's go back to camp. I owe you a good dinner."

12

THAT EVENING, EDWARD AND Charles Sternberg sat in the campaign chairs by the campfire looking across at Red Moon, who preferred his usual cross-legged posture on the dusty earth. Both men sipped on tin cups of coffee, while the shaman on his cup of tea. The conversation, once they had separated themselves from the students and the hired-hands, had covered the outrageous adventures of the day, ending with Red Moon's discovery of what was an obvious fossil site.

All through the recounting, Sternberg sat stoically, barely reacting to even the most visceral descriptions of mayhem and horror. He surprised Edward by seeming to accept every detail of the experience with not even a whit of skepticism. When he had finally reached the end of his narrative, he felt compelled to comment on his colleague's contemplative appearance.

"Charles, have you nothing to say? You sit there as if I've just described a trolley ride on Chestnut Street."

Sternberg regarded him with a gentle half-smile as he struck a match to re-light his pipe. "I am still digesting all that you've told me. It's a fantastical tale, I'll give it that. And if I'd heard it from anyone but you and your Quaker values, I'd not believe a word of it. But I know Edward Cope is a man of high morals. Besides, what benefit would you derive from spinning such a story? The majority of the people in our field would deign you a quack and be done with you, surely you know this. Put simply, you would not risk the ridicule and would never describe such an adventure were you not *forced* to reveal it only because it *is* true."

Edward remained silent for a moment as he considered Sternberg's logic, and had no quarrel with it. "You make good sense," he said. "But, my God, man... Don't you have any questions? Comments? *Anything?*"

Sternberg chuckled, then puffed out a blue cloud. "Oh, I have cartloads. I just haven't got round to them yet."

Edward finished off the last of his coffee. It was bitter and he thought about digging out the bourbon bottle, but discarded the notion. He wanted to be fresh in the morning. "So ask away – it grows late and we want an early start. You'll want to put your crew on Red Moon's find as soon as they're able."

"Agreed." Sternberg paused. "All right, then… You said some of the beasts appeared to have *feathers*…? How do you account for that?"

Edward cleared his throat. "You center on one of the things I've been thinking upon almost constantly. And yes, I am most certain they were feathers, or feather-like, and coupled with the quick movements of the bipedal creatures, it makes me wonder if they are not reptiles at all."

"Really…" Sternberg's response was not a question.

"Quite so. When you factor in the feathers, or even if we must term them *proto*-feathers, I am tempted to say that the dinosaurs are actually forbears of our modern day birds!"

"Meaning they must be warm-blooded…" Sternberg puffed, then: "That is quite a theory."

Edward shook his head. "Not so much a theory as an observation. I've *seen* these beasts, Charles, and they act and look a *lot* like birds."

Red Moon raised his index finger. "I think this. Many times. Yes. Like bird."

Sternberg seemed to consider this for a long pause. "Well, Edward, that is what would be, in paleontological circles, attacked for being not only radical, but absurd. Another vote for you as the worst apostate, a quack of the first mark."

"If you are suggesting I refrain from publishing such heresy, you can be sure I will postulate such ideas before the establishment." Saying this, Edward glanced upward at the evening-to-night sky as the endless play of stars began to emerge. There was magic in that firmament, but it was no match for what he had seen today. He could not care less for what his stodgy colleagues back east might think of what he now knew to be simple fact.

"And then there's the potion itself…" Charles looked pointedly at Red Moon. "That is the one part of the story that truly puzzles me."

"How so?" said Edward.

"Well, assuming we are dealing with phenomena that are ultimately explainable in empirical terms, and that it is not – What? *Magic?* – then I confess to not see the cause and effect of drinking something that has the ability to transport you *anywhere* much less through time." Sternberg paused, re-lit his pipe, then added: "Although more than once enough Kentucky bourbon has transported me to a bed that would not stop spinning!"

They all chuckled at this, even Red Moon.

"Good point, Charles. Especially when you express the issue so succinctly." Edward smoothed his mustache, thought about the bottle of Evan Williams in his tent.

Sternberg leaned in Red Moon's direction. "And so, I fear I must interrogate our red-skinned friend here."

If Red Moon had been offended by the reference, he did not show it as he looked at the man in the bowler hat, awaiting his questions.

"Tell me, Red Moon, what is the function of the potion? What does it really *do?* Must I drink it to actually walk in time?"

There came a pause as Red Moon seemed to be working out how he might explain things with his good, but sometimes limited, vocabulary. Edward had known him long enough to know his new friend truly wanted to get the words right, to get the right meaning out there.

Red Moon held both hands outward, palms up. "Not need for timewalking."

"You don't say!" said Edward. This revelation did not seem to jibe with his experience.

Sternberg's expression brightened as if he were uncovering a secret. "You mean it's just for...for *show?* Theatrics? To get people to see, to notice, I mean."

Red Moon shook his head. "No. Not for...for show. Do two things: make walker not crazy...and let walker *see* where to walk."

Sternberg waved off this explanation. "I don't understand. 'See where to walk'? And that means exactly *what?*"

At that point, Edward interjected, describing the infinite number of dots he had seen and how Red Moon had said they were doors into the past, openings through which they could walk. But Edward had no idea *how* his companion selected the right path.

"You could see them as plainly as the Indian?" Sternberg said, nodding towards Red Moon.

"I think so, but… I didn't know what I was looking at, or what they meant, or where they led."

Sternberg considered this as he puffed his pipe. "But Red Moon most certainly did."

"Oh yes. Rather obvious, isn't it."

Sternberg nodded. "I suppose, yes, it is. But here's an important question: Could someone, say me, 'timewalk' with you if I didn't drink the potion?"

Edward had no answer to that, and remained silent. He looked to Red Moon, who nodded. "Yes. If you close to walker, walker can guide you through. To follow right path, right door."

Sternberg puffed a large cloud into the clear night air. "I should like to do such a thing."

Edward chuckled. "So you say now, sitting here in the safety of a fire and a more temperate time."

Sternberg grinned. "Perhaps. But something I need to do even more quickly is begin to excavate the site you uncovered today. It grows darker and later. Let's retire for the night, gentlemen, and hope tomorrow delivers all we assume it promises."

Edward stood and clasped Sternberg's shoulders. "Thank you, Charles. Thank you for listening to our story and treating it with the respect I believe it deserves."

"As I will continue to do, until you dissuade me otherwise. Goodnight, Edward, and the same to you, Red Moon."

The Indian untangled himself and stood to bid Sternberg a goodnight, then he went to his mare to retrieve his bedclothes. Edward watched him stretch out his blankets beneath the brilliant canopy of stars that formed the ceiling of the Montana Territory, then retired to his tent for a night of sleep punctuated by visions and images of the day before. It was not anything he would term *restful*.

13

AS PROMISED, STERNBERG HAD his team of university students and hired cowboys deployed on the new site at dawn's light. They worked with the precision and energy of a swarm of worker bees, inspired by the urgings of Sternberg that he believed they were on the cusp of a great discovery.

And by the first day's end, the entire team tended to believe him. Edward supervised the last of the work as evening approached, because he had a very strong hunch. Already, they had rescued enough fossils to determine that the remains of two dinosaurs occupied this space, their bones preserved because they had expired in a soft, muddy grave that had hardened over eons to create an almost perfect environment for the preservation of their skeletons.

By some arcane ability, Red Moon had directed Edward's team to the exact location where he'd witnessed firsthand the savage kill and subsequent battle for the carrion. Edward knew he must keep silent before Sternberg's people, but he also knew what they would eventually find as they continued their dig.

And on the third day, Sternberg and his crew had succeeded in separating enough soft sandstone from the almost perfectly preserved bones of *two* dinosaurs to reveal them *in situ*, although still locked halfway into the earth. After another five days of intense work, they had succeeded in clearing beautiful specimens of the skulls of both a *Dryptosaurus* and a hadrosaur that quite possibly had never been classified. Preliminary observation and notes strongly suggested that the dryptosaur had killed the hadrosaur because Sternberg's students had begun comparing teeth-mark impressions that matched up to define an attacker-victim scenario.

The students' work proved indeed correct, although Edward could have saved them a lot of time and trouble since he'd witnessed the event firsthand. He said nothing as he watched the group work for the better part of another week to uncover and retrieve the fossilized skeletons of both creatures almost *in toto*. They would be revered as exquisite museum specimens, and the work of this year's team would be recorded as one of the best in the history of the University of Pennsylvania's many expeditions. Their efforts were amplified when further study revealed the dryptosaur's rib cage and neck vertebrae showed evidence of bite-marks by a *second Dryptosaurus*, suggesting a battle to the death over the scavenged remains.

Although he could not take any direct credit for the papers and presentations that followed, and although he *knew* their informed postulations to be spot-on, Edward chose to contribute to the discussion through a series of sketches which he presented as possible visual interpretations of what Sternberg and his students imagined. His sketchbooks were his way of secretly preserving what he knew to be the most accurate depictions of the great creatures that had come before us.

He averred his drawings may eventually be scoffed at by his peers as being inaccurate, but he knew better, and hoped that posterity might someday prove him correct. But in spite of his convictions, he could not bring himself to draw *feathers* on the predators for fear the resultant laughter would bring his career to a crashing end. While sitting in front of his tent touching up a sketch (without feathers), Red Moon approached him and stood silent, waiting to be recognized.

"Yes, my friend?"

"You and your people very happy with the bones." It was not a question. More a statement of fact, tinged with the pride of responsibility.

Edward smiled. "Oh yes. Very much so."

"You want find more?"

"Well, of course! The season is now more than half done, but yes, more would be wonderful."

Red Moon nodded. "Then…we need walk again."

The idea of going back to that world of almost-constant terror galvanized Edward. The notion had been lurking in the back of his thoughts for weeks and he had been avoiding any consideration of it coming to pass. "Are you sure? Did you not point out the smallest evidence of a fossil when we first met?"

Red Moon dismissed him with a wave of his hand. "I know that place from other walking. Before you find me."

"I understand."

"You want new bones, we must walk again."

Edward paused to think on the suggestion. Of *course* he wanted "new bones." He would always want more bones, but at what price to his sanity, his well-being? As the weeks had passed since his bout with abject terror, he had begun to downgrade the event in terms of its true peril. But the idea of returning to that time as a real possibility, a real choice, filled him with dread. And yet, he knew it could be a surefire way to locate new fossils.

"Let me think on it," he said finally. "I will tell you my decision in the morning."

14

"DO WE REALLY NEED to drink this foul mixture?" Edward regarded the wooden bowl containing the ritualistic potion. They sat next to each other, by the coals of the morning campfire, as his friend offered it to him. Having learned the true nature of the preparation, based on his previous experience, Edward did not believe it would help keep him calm or more in control of himself.

Red Moon frowned. "Drink, Edward Cope. No harm you do it."

Edward shrugged, held the bowl in both hands, and poured it down his throat as quickly as possible. "I don't know why I need to see all those specks as long as I am holding on for the ride."

"No matter. Now we walk."

They had traveled south of their last position and into a canyon that perhaps had been a river valley eons ago. Places where water once existed proved to be prime locations for the process of fossilization. As Edward followed Red Moon's lead over the rough, uneven terrain, he once again sensed his peripheral vision begin to halo and shimmer at the outermost edges. The potion, doing its job.

"I see. Good place. We go now. Hold." Red Moon turned and grasped Edward's forearm as they stepped forward – and, ultimately, *backward* – into a long-ago earth.

The first thing he noticed, as before, was the low-level thrum of insects and the skittering of things across the forest floor. And of course the shadowy *green* of everything. There was no evidence of the canyon from which they had exited. Instead, a wide serene river flowed along the verdant banks where they stood. The body of water stretched so distant, it could have easily been an inland sea, if not for the subtle flow of current.

As before, Edward required more than a moment to orient himself with the reality of his timewalking. Leaning forward, hands on his knees, he had paused to take several deep breaths when Red Moon nudged his shoulder.

"Edward Cope. Look." He pointed downriver to a group of quadrupeds, distinctive by their long necks, thick bodies and legs, and long tails.

"A herd!" said Edward. "I have often imagined such animals traveled in groups, and now I am seeing it for myself. Amazing!"

"They calm. No danger," said Red Moon. "We go closer."

"Yes, yes... Lead the way."

Edward followed his friend along the shoreline, only pausing to venture inland a few yards to avoid a crocodilian beast feeding on a carcass of unknown identity. But other than that, their foray into the terror-laden world remained relatively safe. As they closed in on the group of long-necks, Edward observed that the largest of the beasts were no larger than a modern Indian elephant, and many of the herd appeared to be either dwarves or juveniles. The animals were herbivores, preferring to wade in the shallows of the river, with occasional forays into the forest to graze on fronds and tender shoots of vegetation. They moved with a slow grace and appeared to be as gentle as a lamb or baby calf. Edward felt no fear from them, and when he and Red Moon drew ever closer, the long-necks took little notice of their presence.

It was at that moment Edward noticed why the herd of long-necks had crowded together near the bank of the river: the swollen body of one of their members lay on its side, its great bulk shuddering and its snake-like neck trying to look upward. Watching the beast labor to right itself, to gain its feet, Edward surmised this animal would never rise again. Even though he saw no evidence of an attack, the long-neck appeared stricken in some fashion. Every time it tried to roll over to stand, it failed, emitting a honking bleat shot through with pain and helplessness.

"It's dying," said Edward. "Something's wrong with it."

Red Moon tugged at his sleeve. "We lucky. See enough. Go back before trouble."

Edward looked from the fallen long-neck in the shallows to the dense forest to their left. Despite the serene tableau before them, his limited experience told him something hungry could burst forth at any moment. To Red Moon he said: "Yes. You're right. We know enough. We *can* go back now."

Turning, Red Moon indicated the proper path and Edward followed it to the letter as they retraced their steps along the shoreline. He loved the idea that they could leave this dangerous era so quickly and yet have valuable information regarding a possible fossil site.

As they pushed through the dense undergrowth to emerge in a stand of rail-like proto-conifers, the forest thinned-out, allowing Edward to see a greater distance in all directions. It was comforting to be able to move along and not feel so totally enclosed by the thick vegetation. When he walked through such places, his skin crawled with the fear and expectation that a predator could lurk just yards away and remain undetected.

"We close now." Red Moon's words yanked him from his thoughts.

A honking roar pierced the tropic stillness, a sound which spoke of hunger and great ferocity.

"*How* close? Something is out there! Close to us!"

"Not far. This way." Pointing off to his right, Red Moon moved with stealth and confidence and his unerringly canny ability to navigate through time and place.

Edward matched him step for step until his friend held up his right hand signaling a pause, a stop. Edward did so just as he noticed movement in the distance through the sparse stand of trees. At first he could only discern a splash of colors – reds, greens, pale yellows – but then the splash became resolved into the moving bulk of something large and agile.

"What's that?" said Edward, pointing off to his right.

Red Moon did not reply, but turned on his heel to regard the beast passing their position as it homed in on the long-neck herd they had just witnessed.

"Oh my God in Heaven!" The words rushed out of Edward in a harsh half-whisper. Although obscured by distance and the variegated trees, he saw enough: thick, muscled hind legs, a thrashing tail, a massive head crowned with bright feathers, and open jaws studded with countless dagger-teeth. And for good measure, twice the size of the dryptosaurs he'd seen on his last visit to hell.

The sight of the nightmare creature had held him mid-stride, and it was not till Red Moon gripped his arm that he broke the paralysis of abject fear. "We go. *Now.*"

They took one more step forward and Edward found himself in the dry, sere surroundings of Montana in late summer, 1876. Although he knew he was safe now, Edward could not shake the memory of the last vision he'd seen before returning to his own time. A predator of such size could only be one creature, and although only jaw and thigh fragments had been unearthed at this point and so far unidentified, his rival Charles Marsh had extrapolated upon the nature of such a meat-eater. Marsh had proclaimed that when he found more complete fossils of this upright, bipedal carnivore, he would name it *Allosaurus*, which in Latin meant "different lizard," because it was certainly *that*.

Edward allowed himself a small smile as he smoothed the ends of his mustache. Charles Marsh may predict the glory of his uncovering of an *Allosaurus*, but Edward basked in the knowledge that he'd already *seen* one. Such were his thoughts as he and Red Moon returned to the encampment for rest and sustenance.

When evening settled in and the hot, dry temperatures of the day dissipated, Edward convened the now-expected meeting of himself, Sternberg, and Red Moon. After he related the experiences of his second "walk," Sternberg spoke in a soft voice as he prepared a new bowl of tobacco in his pipe.

"We're almost finished with the *Dryptosaurus* – the skull is magnificent. I hate to wrap it up for transport just yet because I so much enjoy just looking at it."

"Then don't!" said Edward. "We aren't packing for Cheyenne tomorrow."

Sternberg nodded, continued. "We can at least begin to examine the long-neck site by late afternoon tomorrow…as long as you are certain your friend can locate it."

"I will find it," said Red Moon. "It…it comes to me."

Sternberg ignited his pipe, drew and puffed. "Yes, I am quite well aware of your ability. I look forward to your revelations."

Red Moon said nothing, and Edward suspected his friend did not always understand everything Charles uttered, and didn't care one way or the other.

When no one else spoke, Sternberg continued. "I'm curious about the beast you saw on your exit. Could it be the animal Marsh has predicted?"

Edward thought for a moment, tempted to say anything which might deprecate his bothersome nemesis, then nodded. "Loathe as I am to admit it, yes. It could very well be. I only saw it for scant seconds, but that was enough for any man. Its size! Its speed! Something hardly imagined. And the *colors* of the predators such as this monster are so unexpected. They must be males because the use of color to attract females is something we still see today in all the ornithological species."

Sternberg chuckled. "Ah, there you go down the bird path once again."

"If you ever see them, you will not be such a skeptic. It's undeniable."

"Yes," said Red Moon. "Very much like birds."

"Well, that's all well and good, but unless we ever find a fossil with feathers, I think you need to keep this kind of knowledge close to your vest. The common belief is that dinosaurs are giant lizards."

Edward nodded. "As was my own belief…until I saw them with my own eyes!"

Sternberg waved a dismissive hand. "You don't need to convince me. I have no doubt we stand at the threshold of information that would surely stand paleontology on its head. But the iconoclast is always an easy target."

Retrieving his pocket watch, Edward glanced down upon it. "If we wish an early start to find the new site, then the hour is upon us, gentlemen."

"Agreed," said Sternberg as he stood and re-seated his bowler on his head. "Good night, Edward, and to you, Red Moon."

Worn out from the wonder and insanity of another "walk," Edward was grateful to see Sternberg depart. Red Moon had already prepared his sleeping gear and settled down within. Edward regarded him and shook his head slowly.

"Do you think me and my people are crazy for what we do?"

"No." Red Moon's expression belied no feeling or intention.

Edward grinned. "Good. Just because you feel indebted to me, I would never want you to feel you were helping me against your will."

"It is my honor to help the one who brought me back to life."

"Thank you, but I feel I am just…using you. Is there anything I can do for you?"

Red Moon considered this, then: "Someday, I think I like see your village, this Phil A-dell-fia. I like to see place where you send bones."

Edward felt a swelling in his chest. He smiled broadly. "That is wonderful! As much as I would love to show it all to you. I promise I will try to make it so."

He shook hands with his friend and bid him goodnight.

15

TRUE TO HIS WORD, Red Moon and Edward led Sternberg's crew into the nearby canyon and pointed to an unlikely location where their dig should begin. An upward sloping wall of limestone and talus that gave no clues as to what may lie beneath, but the students and range-hands attacked it with the aplomb and experience gained from almost two months of field work.

Within two hours, the bones of a dinosaur began to take shape from the surrounding earth that had imprisoned it. Edward had been present for the morning dig, and when the first traces of linked vertebrae suggested something with a long neck, he knew Red Moon had been true to form. He smiled as he recalled seeing the animal just yesterday – even the notion of such a thing seemed absurd, and yet it was true. From that experience, he was quite certain he had unearthed a new, as-yet-unnamed species of long-necks. He was certain it did not belong to Marsh's *Brontosaurus* genus because even the adult males of the herd were nowhere near as large. He practically beamed with the knowledge that he would be able to proclaim an altogether new species of long-necks and have the honor of naming it.

As the dig continued, Edward retired to his tent to sketch out from memory a scene of the herd of long-necks. The sketchbooks contained other pages of his renderings of the creatures seen during his sojourns back into time. He had made them as accurate as possible, including the proto-feathers he had seen on the carnivores, for his own personal papers, as a matter of accurate record. He would never consider them for public release. Red Moon had taken his leave to visit his village to the northwest, promising to return by nightfall. The hours passed as Edward worked diligently to recreate what he had seen while "walking." But as the hour approached 4:00 p.m., he was interrupted by Zeke Hardesty, calling his name excitedly.

"Doc! Doc! Ya gotta see this! Doc!"

Before Edward could arise from his chair, the front flap of his tent flew back to reveal the grizzled, unshaven face of Zeke, his eyes wide.

"What is it, man?!" Edward hoped his tone carried the indignation he was feeling. Zeke barging in like that was a show of great disrespect. "How dare you—!"

"Doc, I am *so* sorry, but I spied some riders heading this way from the east."

"How many?"

"Looks like just two… But you ain't expectin' nobody, are ya?"

"No. How far?"

"At least a half-hour. They ain't ridin' hard."

"Are you certain they are headed in our direction?"

"Looks that way. Could be followin' our wagon ruts…"

"Indians?"

"Too far to tell just yet."

"Come with me," said Edward, who exited his tent and walked to his horse, where he retrieved the brass spyglass from his saddlebag. He handed it to the cowboy. "Take this. Tell me what you see."

"Gotcha!" Zeke grabbed the instrument and ran off towards the main encampment and his tethered horse.

There was a rise on the south side of the Judith, and Edward expected his man would ride there for the best vantage point. He debated whether he should wait here for a report from Zeke, or head out to the dig site and alert Sternberg of approaching strangers. The idea of someone heading straight-on to his camp was unsettling, although he could not discount the possibility that the riders could be travelers in need. The Montana Territory could be a harsh and unforgiving place for those not familiar with its demands. And people who had become lost or disoriented could very well decide to follow the path of wagon wheel impressions in the hopes of them eventually leading to a safe haven.

With that thought firmly in mind, Edward decided to await word from Zeke in the case he might be needed. Even though he was not a medical doctor, he possessed a fair degree of knowledge regarding anatomy and basic first aid. That said, he hoped his minimal skills would not be necessary.

Returning to his sketchbook, he worked on a new page until he heard the shouts of Zeke's approach, the gallop of his horse, and the sound of his dismount. "Doc! You in there? Hey!"

As he emerged from his tent, he saw the bow-legged cowboy, spyglass in his left hand, converging on him.

"Did that thing help?"

"Hellfire, yes! I gotta get me one of these things."

"Yes, I'm sure. Would you be so kind as to tell what or who you saw through its tube?"

Zeke guffawed. "Oh, yeah… Two men. White men. One feller with a beard and an eastern hat… The other's a cowboy, and he looks like none other than Black Dan McKay!"

Edward did not speak as he processed this. A beard and an eastern hat; Edward knew immediately who approached his camp. The audacity! Marsh and his henchman. How dare he!?

"Still headed in our direction, I presume?"

Zeke nodded. "Dead on."

"How long before they arrive?"

"Fifteen minutes, I reckon."

Edward nodded. Not much time. "Head out to the dig and tell Sternberg what's going on. Tell him Marsh is on his way *here*. Tell him to join me as soon as possible."

"You betcha, Doc."

Watching his rowdy head west toward the canyon site, Edward re-seated his hat, smoothed his mustache, and walked towards the main encampment where Marsh would eventually appear. He could not imagine what might be the cause of this occasion. Was Marsh in trouble? Lost? Attacked by Indians? Or, knowing his adversary quite well, did Edward suspect him of some low motive? Most likely.

The late afternoon sun would soon be cresting the foothills, a sign for Thibodeaux to begin preparations for the evening meal. As he emerged from his tent wearing his long canvas apron, Edward met him and told him to plan on two extra plates for dinner.

"And who might they be?" said the cook.

Edward nodded sadly. "You shall see soon enough. Just be warned, Frenchy."

"I am so warned." The cook turned toward his wagon and his panoply of skillets and pots, then turned for a look back at Edward. "Shall I prepare something special?"

Edward grinned. "Absolutely *not.*"

The minutes ticked past with an agonizing slowness, despite an almost constant checking of his pocket watch – or perhaps *because* of it. The braying of Sternberg's mule reached him, and he turned to see his trusted colleague astride the animal in its resolute approach. Directly behind him loped Zeke and his mare.

"Did Zeke tell me rightly?" he said.

"If he told you Marsh will be here any minute, then yes."

Sternberg reined the mule to a stop, slid off her back. "Incredible! Something's afoot, Edward. Of that I can tell you."

"Yes, that thought has occurred to me as well."

"What do you intend?"

"I like to think I am a gentleman, Charles. And to that end, I will receive him as a guest and treat him as such until he gives me reason to not do so."

Sternberg chuckled. "As I suspected. But that Marsh is a sly one. I cannot imagine him paying a genial social call. He's going to want to know what success, if any, you've enjoyed, that's for certain."

"No doubt. And he won't be learning very much about that, I assure you."

They both shared a brief laugh, then Edward addressed Zeke: "Head out to the eastern end of camp and greet our impending visitors."

"*What* kind? What's an 'impendin'?"

"It's not your concern. Just do it."

Adjusting the gun and holster that rested on his right thigh, Zeke nodded, gently prodded his horse's flank, then directed her toward the camp's eastern entrance. Edward and Sternberg followed on foot. The cowboy hadn't gotten halfway to his post when the two riders appeared downslope toward the river basin. No doubt about their identities. Marsh, astride a white stallion, wore a tan field jacket over a white shirt and bow tie, cinched by baggy trousers to accommodate his considerable girth. He wore a rumpled, dust-laden pork-pie hat which did nothing to compliment his round face and unkempt bushy beard. His henchman appeared in every way his opposite. Tall and lean, his angular face clean-shaven, defined by raven-dark eyes and a lopsided smile punctuated by a gold incisor tooth. True to his name, Dan McKay dressed all in black, from his boots to his rakish hat.

Edward watched as Zeke intercepted their progress on the edge of camp. "Good evening, fellers. My boss sent me out here to welcome the two of you."

"Very thoughtful of him," said Marsh. "Would you be so kind as to lead us into your encampment?"

Turning his horse slowly around, Zeke did so.

Standing alongside Sternberg, Edward waited until Marsh and McKay pulled up their mounts a yard or so before them. Then he addressed his rival: "Charles Othniel Marsh... I must confess I would have never expected such a moment as this. What brings you to my expedition, as if I cannot guess?"

Marsh eased off his horse with more than a little clumsy effort. His field jacket bulged about his middle, and Edward could not help but notice the increased weight gain since last they'd met. Marsh touched the brim of his battered hat, mimicked a parody of a bow, and smiled through his beard. "It appears my...*agent* encountered yours at the Black Hills Depot, and when I deduced we were indeed both within hailing distance, I thought it would be beneficial for the two of us to have a civilized evening together in the midst of a most *un*civilized part of the country."

Edward smiled. "That is most thoughtful of you, Doctor Marsh. Or should I call you by the moniker your Yalie sycophants prefer: '*Uncle Otty*'?"

Marsh stiffened and bristled at the jibe, but remained civil. "*Charles* will be sufficient."

"Very well," said Edward. "And now introductions all around. You both know my man Zeke... And I am quite certain my able assistant, Charles Sternberg, is known in paleontological circles..."

Marsh nodded as he looked at Sternberg. "You studied under Professor Benjamin Mudge at Kansas State, did you not?"

"Yes, I did, Professor."

"Good man, Mudge. I trust he prepared you well for our fools-errand profession."

Sternberg grinned. "Most thoroughly."

A silence followed as Edward, Sternberg, and Zeke all stared at McKay.

Marsh could not help but notice the awkward gap in the conversation and moved to fill it. "My *faux pas*, gentlemen. Please welcome my agent and assistant, Daniel Jacob McKay."

As if on cue, Black Dan leaned to his left and slid off his saddle to assume a wide-legged stance with such oleaginous skill, Edward felt a chill pass through him. The man's actions and appearance suggested nothing but danger and peril. He wore a gunbelt at a rakish angle so that his holstered six-shooter dangled almost at the same length as his right arm.

"Pleased to meet you, Mr. McKay." Edward extended his right hand and McKay took in a brief, heavy shake. Edward looked back to Marsh. "Your timing was quite good, Charles. We are about to convene and break for the evening meal, of which you and your 'agent' are welcome to join."

16

THIBODEAUX OUTDID HIMSELF WITH the jackrabbit stew with rice balls and beans in a light cooking sherry sauce. Perhaps in no small measure because of the good food, everyone remained civil and congenial throughout the meal. Marsh carried much of the conversation with boorish anecdotes designed to ultimately make him look good as a scholar, mentor, and of course bone hunter. Black Dan said little other than *Pass the salt*, and sat at his plate with a sullen, wary expression. Edward endured it all, wondering what truly motivated his rival to boldly enter his camp.

As plates were cleared, Marsh gave a sign to McKay, who stood and went to his horse to retrieve something from a saddlebag. Watching him with a surreptitious eye, Edward wondered what trickery Marsh had planned, and found himself a bit chagrined to see McKay carry forth a bottle of whiskey.

As the gunman entered the circle of men, Marsh clapped his hands together and smiled. "Ah ha, gentlemen! And now we come to the best part of the evening, where we all join in conviviality to celebrate our mutual passions!"

"That's quite thoughtful of you, Charles."

"Nothing less than you would do in similar circumstances, Edward!" Marsh took the bottle from McKay and held it up at if a trophy. "I bring you a special treat from Tullahoma, Tennessee: George Dickel sour mash whiskey. His distillery is causing quite a stir in Kentucky because it rivals the best bourbons to come from that state."

"I've heard tell," said Sternberg. "You can't call a whiskey 'bourbon' if it's not distilled in Kentucky. Is that true?"

Marsh nodded. "True enough. I suppose that's why Dickel calls his 'sour mash,' but I can assure you, gentlemen, there's nothing sour about this nectar!"

Thibodeaux appeared with tin cups for the four men, and gave each a generous pour of several fingers. When each was served, Marsh raised his cup in a toast. "To many years of congenial rivalry, and that there's enough bones underground to satisfy us all!"

Everyone tipped back their cup, savoring the truly fine whiskey. After two more rounds, Marsh stood and approached Edward. "All right, my colleague, you must know I am curious about your season. Have you found anything important?"

Edward shook his head as if in reprimand. "The true motive for your visit...finally revealed."

Marsh stroked his beard, smiled impishly through it. "Am I to be convicted of being inquisitive?"

Before Edward could answer, Marsh moved away from the epicenter of the evening fire and homed in on one of the buck wagons which held crated specimens ready for transport. A canvas tarp covered the nearest one, and Marsh tore it aside with a flourish. "Let's have a look, shall we?!"

"Hey!" Edward yelled. "That's out of line!"

But Marsh acted as if he heard nothing as his gaze became fixed upon a pristine skull of a *Dryptosaurus*. "My God, he is simply magnificent! I've never seen a fossil in such perfect condition."

Grabbing the tarp, Edward pulled it back into place, covering the skull. "Well, now you have. But I must ask you to cease this behavior, Charles. It is unseemly and unprofessional."

"Perhaps I had a bit more mash than I should have. I offer my apologies. But seeing that specimen cannot help but remind me of your original name for such a fearsome predator."

Edward said nothing, ignoring Marsh's effort to embarrass him. All things considered, he remained a wholly unlikeable man.

"The hour grows late, and we all have work in the morning."

"Ushering us out, are you?"

"It is late, Charles."

"Where are you digging these days?"

"Somewhere west of here. I couldn't show you in the dark even if I wanted to…and I most assuredly do *not*."

Marsh nodded, fingers combing through his unruly beard. "Still keeping that sketchbook?"

"Certainly."

"I've always envied your talent in that regard. Any chance I could have a look-see?"

"Not even a scant one."

Marsh nodded again and moved slowly back to the fire where Sternberg and McKay sat staring at one another. "Time to vamoose, Danny Boy. You sure you can find our way home?"

McKay rubbed his chin and smiled, revealing his gold incisor. The tooth gleamed in the firelight. "Moon should be up soon. Plenty to see by. And my compass never lets me down."

As Edward escorted them to their horses, the soft sound of approaching hooves in the dark gave everyone pause. McKay tilted back the brim of his black hat and quickly rested his right hand on the pearl handle of his low-slung Colt. "Who's there?"

As if in answer, Red Moon emerged from the darkness beyond the range of the fire. He pulled up his horse's progress and sat silently waiting to see what should be his appropriate action.

"May I introduce you to our guide, Red Moon."

Marsh looked with raised eyebrows from the Indian to Edward. "From what I heard, your boys couldn't find a guide at the depot."

"That is true. We encountered Red Moon from a nearby Crow settlement."

Marsh tilted his head as he looked back at Red Moon, who was tying up his mount at a nearby wagon. "Well, that was certainly fortunate, was it not?"

"Fortune is fickle. But sometimes she smiles." Edward cleared his throat. "Now, good night, Charles. Perhaps I will see you back east after the season is at an end."

"If we are invited to the same event, no doubt. Especially if we have important news to present. I know *I* do!"

Sternberg picked up the bottle of Dickel sour mash and held it out for the professor, who waved it off. "Keep it, lads. Plenty more where that came from!"

Edward watched them mount up and ease their horses into the eastern darkness. Moments later the first pale glimmers of a moonrise to the north cleared the higher terrain above the river basin. Black Dan had been correct. Red Moon joined Edward and Sternberg, but said nothing.

"Well, that was…*strange*," said Sternberg.

"Yes. From beginning to end. Clearly a hunting expedition. I don't trust him a lick."

"Who this man?" said Red Moon.

Edward recounted a brief history of Marsh and his relationship with him. Red Moon evinced true surprise that more than one man would want to dig up bones, but he accepted it with his usual stoicism. Finally he said: "So…we tell him nothing."

Sternberg chuckled. "Less than nothing!"

"He seemed suspicious about the 'guide' business, didn't you think?"

Sternberg shrugged. "Possibly. But Marsh can have no idea what we have going on. Knowing him, he probably thought our sending Zeke to the depot was a ruse of some sort."

Edward chuckled at that notion. "We are simply not that clever, nor do we want to be."

"Do you have tomorrow's day planned?" Sternberg held the bottle of sour mash in both hands as if a precious infant. "And do we have time for a night cap?"

"I'd like to get both sites completely exposed plus have one more 'walk' with Red Moon. And yes, after that bizarre evening, a capper is in order."

Sternberg grinned as he poured single fingers for the three of them.

17

DESPITE THE LATE HOUR of the night before, Sternberg had his crews up and off to the digs at the usual hour. Edward figured to stop by both locations before he and Red Moon attempted to find one more optimal fossil bed. Because of the Indian's unique ability, Edward's season had already achieved monumental success and the University of Pennsylvania, as well as the Drexel Academy of Natural Sciences, would be overjoyed to see their funding of his expedition paying such marvelous dividends.

As he turned in his breakfast plate, he signaled for Zeke and Harley to join him.

When they did, he told them not to accompany Sternberg's parties.

"You want us to stay back? Here?" said Zeke. "I thought we was ta watch over the two digs?"

"You are, but I have a funny feeling about Marsh being here last night. I need you to lay back in camp until Red Moon and I are safely away. And then you and Harley can split up for both dig sites."

"Sure, Doc. That's easy if'n that's what you prefer."

"It is. Just stay out of sight until you see us on our way, unhindered."

Zeke hocked up an early-morning wad of tobacco juice, hurled it back beyond his left shoulder, then flashed a brown-toothed smile. "Easy money," he said.

"I hope so, Zeke. I truly do."

With that, Edward turned away from them and headed for his tent for a few items needed for the day's adventure. He smiled at the idea of calling what they planned merely an "adventure." More like an impossible journey into the most nightmarish place ever conceived. A place brimming over with life…and quick, savage death. Every moment spent in that time tempted fate, and as terrifying as it may be, Edward could not resist one last visit in the hope of locating one more spectacular fossil site.

When he reached the horses, where Red Moon stood waiting by the mare and the roan, he dropped a full canteen, his sketchbook, and his spyglass into his saddlebag.

"Ready to go?"

Red Moon nodded. "Ready."

Mounting up, Edward followed his companion out of camp and into the foothills. He rode warily, watching for any sign of Marsh or McKay, but saw nothing. They reached the cave where Red Moon laid out his preparations and Edward started a small fire in the circle of stones from their previous visit. He watched as Red Moon prepared the potion with meticulous care until it was finally time to drink from the wooden bowl. Soon he was feeling the effects of its arcane ingredients. The shimmering in the periphery, the distended distance, and the intensity of colors in even the dullest rocks – all disorienting but no longer a cause for anxiety.

"We go," said Red Moon.

"I didn't tell you," said Edward, "but I would like to go to a place, a time where we might see that same creature we saw last. Is that possible?"

"The big fast one? Many teeth?"

"Yes. Could we, I mean, *you* find him or one like him again?"

"Yes, but…you sure you want be near something like that?"

"Well, preferably I would like to find a *dead* one that we could dig up. So far only fragments of that beast have been unearthed. To find a complete one would be a sensation."

Red Moon said nothing, appeared to be considering this. Then: "We go. See."

They rode deeper into the river basin to a point where it widened considerably, flanked by steep walls of limestone. Dismounting, they tethered their horses to a cottonwood. Edward saw specks of color and light everywhere – an infinity of pathways, so said Red Moon, who now pointed at one of them. Just as they prepared to step forward, a voice intruded on the silence that had held them. Loud, distant, and full of menace.

"Why don't we just hold it right there!"

Red Moon made a move to step forward, but Edward held him back. "Wait!"

Turning to the direction of the voice, he saw Dan McKay standing next to a boulder more than fifty yards from them. Despite his precautions with Zeke and Harley, Edward realized he had tried to match wits with a truly competent and dangerous fellow. McKay held a Remington rifle at his shoulder, sighted directly at Edward's head. Maintaining his aim, rifle at his shoulder and squinting eye, McKay advanced on their position, closing the distance between them quickly.

"Don't move. This man is a killer," said Edward, fighting against the effects of the potion.

"You bet yer life on that one," said Dan. He lowered the rifle in his left hand while drawing his Colt six-shooter with his right.

"What do you want, McKay?"

"Not *you*, that's for sure."

Edward looked at Black Dan as he smiled a big wide ugly smile. His gold tooth flashed in the midmorning sunlight, and Edward wondered how many men had seen that glinting incisor as the last thing they ever saw in this life. "I don't think I understand."

While McKay kept his six-shooter trained upon Edward's forehead, he directed a glance at Red Moon. "It's *him* I'm wantin'."

"What?! For Marsh? In God's name, *why?!*"

"Don't rightly know, but I'm figurin' he thinks this savage is helpin' you too much. But you know what? I don't rightly give a good fuck *why*. Marsh pays me good and that's all that means much to me."

"I— I can't believe this!" Edward felt such total outrage, he fought an urge to attack the gunslinger with his bare hands, something he knew would be fatal. He felt so helpless, so inadequate to the situation.

In a simple, practiced, fluid motion, McKay flipped the Remington over his right shoulder and sheathed it in a scabbard-like holster across his back. Then, with his left hand now free, McKay grabbed Red Moon by the upper arm. "Time to come with me, Chief," he said over a wide grin.

In that precise moment of contact, Red Moon placed his thin spidery hand on McKay's as he moved forward with unexpected agility, also reaching out to touch Edward. The effect was all three men pitching forward—

—into another time, instantly immersed into a deeply green, buzzing, screaming, humid, alien place.

McKay reeled, spun, and cried out in abject shock. Losing his grip on Red Moon, the gunman found himself in an impossible place. The hard, dry Montana landscape had vanished in a single blink of an eye and he stood in the midst of an overwhelming forest of impossible *green*.

Edward and Red Moon, prepared for the instantaneous transition, broke free of McKay and ran headlong through the dense undergrowth.

"That was spectacular! Where are we?!" Edward shouted as he half-stumbled forward.

"Not know for sure. Close, maybe."

Edward was not certain what his friend meant by his reply, but he knew their first order was to put some distance between themselves and McKay. Something screamed over their heads and Edward looked up to see a pterosaur swooping down to investigate them. Red Moon ducked and pulled Edward under the fronds of a large proto-fern.

"Look," said Red Moon, pointing back in the direction where they had left McKay.

Edward followed his friend's pointing finger and saw the gunman holding his Colt revolver straight out at arm's length, turning, half-hopping in circles to cover his entire perimeter. His expression was a mixture of terror and disbelief as he tried to resolve the reality of the time and place into which he'd been yanked.

"If I weren't as terrified as him," said Edward, "I'd want to laugh. Just look at that poor bastard. He doesn't know what to think."

They watched McKay from their dense cover. He stood no more than twenty yards from their position, but he had no idea where they might be. Overhead, the inquisitive pterosaur returned and angled down upon him. Panicked, McKay fired off several pistol rounds at the flying dinosaur.

Edward could not contain a burst of laughter. The *fool!*

The explosive reports of the revolver stirred up the fauna. The forest floor practically vibrated with skittering, chittering sounds of myriad footfalls and chirps and cries of the smaller but equally hardy and dangerous denizens of this place. McKay heard the increase in the ambient noise and must have known his gunshots had been the impetus for the sudden increase in activity.

"Cope!" His cry into the chaos spoke of his terror and total lack of understanding. "Where are you?! Help!"

Edward watched as McKay continually spun, his revolver in his outstretched hand, trying to scan his entire perimeter. Another hideous scream pierced the thick, tropical air. Something had encountered a frightful death. This was followed by a triumphant, honking roar.

McKay swiped his sleeve across his face, clearing the copious sweat from his eyes. His expression reflected sheer, unvarnished panic. He didn't know if he should advance through the forest to find a less vulnerable position, or remain in place. And then in the midst of the idiot thrum of life in the lush vegetation all around him, he tilted his head to listen to a new sound.

Watching the gunslinger, Edward heard the sound as well. A thrashing, crashing of limbs and fronds. Something was moving through the dense forest. Something large. Something fast. Something moving toward their position.

McKay must have sensed this, because he turned and pushed his way through the thick undergrowth, running blindly away from the onrushing sound of something converging on the scene like the approach of an out-of-control steam locomotive. Edward and McKay remained hunkered down beneath the fronds of a giant fern-like tree, listening to the sound of a great beast closing in on them and watching McKay run blindly straight towards them. Whatever the beast, it was coming up from behind the fleeing gunman in black.

Another ear-splitting roar rolled through the forest, and thirty yards behind McKay the trees exploded apart as something from the worst of nightmares broke past them. Edward knew it was the same beast he'd fleetingly glimpsed upon their last exit: the most fearsome predator paleontologists had so far discovered.

For a moment, they stared at one another, unmoving, the gunslinger and the *Allosaurus* – eight tons of killing machine. From head to tail it was more than thirty feet long, and it towered above them at a height of twenty-five feet. Its hind legs, thick pylons rippling with corded muscle beneath a slick, polished hide mottled in yellows, reds, and browns. Its forelimbs twitched, closing its three-digit claws instinctively at the sight of prey. Its huge head, weighing perhaps a half-ton, tilted slowly so it could study, with bulging green eyes, the odd biped stooped before it. Edward could not take his gaze from the magnificent monster; it stood in life beyond all the imaginings of Marsh and his colleagues. No one had described anything so terrifying as this *Allosaurus*. Its lower jaw hung open, dripping saliva, displaying rows of dagger-teeth, and its throat heaved to the furious beat of its breath. The nightmare head dipped and bobbed and weaved and suddenly the giant jaws snapped shut as if in anticipation of its next meal.

Then it raised that frightful head, nostrils flaring, testing the air, smelling the new human smells. When it made this move, McKay broke free from his paralysis of pure terror. Reaching over his shoulder, he retrieved his Remington and fired two quick shots into the exposed throat of the carnivore. This show of bravery shocked Edward. The man was standing his ground in the face of a true monster.

The *Allosaurus* bellowed as the slugs pierced its flesh, then dropped its head level with its attacker, extending its tail almost straight, horizontal with the ground. The great legs moved, and it surged forward in several huge strides, but McKay held his ground, firing three more rounds into the great head. One of the slugs penetrated its right eye, which exploded in a spray of glistening tissue. The dinosaur screamed, then shot forward with alarming speed, its jaws wide open, and into that maw, McKay emptied the remainder of his rifle's magazine.

Edward watched the confrontation practically in disbelief. It was inconceivable that any man, when the chips were down, could face down such a ravaging carnivore, but Black Dan belied the notion. The impact of the bullets entering the beast's skull through the roof of its mouth must have had some effect. It stumbled forward, its headlong charge suddenly looking clumsy and uncontrolled. Pausing to turret its hideous head to see McKay with its good eye, its tail thrashed and its foreclaws trembled. Obviously, the fusillade had effected some damage.

Dropping the empty rifle, McKay used the momentary pause to retreat and draw his six-shooter. His heavy cowboy boots did not make running an easy task, but he put some distance between himself and the *Allosaurus*. The angle of his retreat took him within ten yards of where Edward and Red Moon lay hidden, and then the gunman was past them.

At the same time, the *Allosaurus* lurched forward, swinging its terrible head from side to side as if to shake off the effects of the bullets. The effort seemed to be working as it suddenly burst past Edward and Red Moon and accelerated towards the two-legged thing that had inflicted such harm on it.

Edward watched the beast pass their position with surprising agility. He had lost sight of McKay, but heard a sudden volley of loud gunshots from his six-shooter. Four shots in rapid succession. Another bellow from the *Allosaurus* rattled through the forest.

At that moment, Red Moon tugged at Edward's sleeve. "Not good here. We go."

"I agree!" said Edward, standing up with great caution.

Red Moon joined him, placed a hand on Edward's elbow, and steered him from the cover of the fronds to a spot very close to the trunk of a thick bald cypress. Another step forward and they had walked back to present-day Montana. Edward blinked, smiled, gulped in a deep breath of the warm dry air. What an incredible transformation! He would never take Red Moon's magical ability for granted.

"We safe now," said his friend.

"Yes. Unlike McKay."

Red Moon nodded. "He not part our time. No more."

"No doubt about that," said Edward as he followed Red Moon across the basin toward their horses still tethered to the cottonwood.

18

A WEEK PASSED BEFORE the expedition began digging out the most recent site. Deep in the flatlands of the Judith River basin, Edward had selected what would mostly likely be the last dig of the summer. Aided by Red Moon, Edward had directed his people to begin a blind excavation into the limestone deposits with no real indication of what may lie beneath the rocks. Within two days, Sternberg's number one team had uncovered the first traces of the leg and foot bones of an animal of considerable size. Two more days of careful chipping and dusting revealed what promised to be a largely intact skeleton of an impossibly large carnivore. When a week had passed, Sternberg was practically ecstatic when he proclaimed the dig would be unearthing the first fully preserved, intact fossil of Marsh's *Allosaurus*. His rival may have named it, but he was going to be the one who presented it to the modern world fully formed.

It was at that point Edward became more thoroughly involved in the dig. Red Moon, by some arcane ability, had directed his team to the place he had witnessed in another time. He knew now not to question it, but to simply deal with it. The University of Pennsylvania students expressed surprise when they saw their professor down on his knees joining in on the hot, hard work of exposing the past. Edward dismissed their concerns by telling them he always participated in the last dig of the season, and assured them the discovery of the *Allosaurus* fossils would be a fitting capstone to the 1876 expedition.

Despite such flummery to his students, Edward knew full well why he had immersed himself in the final days of the excavation of the *Allosaurus* skeleton. He knew what else may lie within the yielding limestone of the site.

And three days later, as Sternberg had his charges busy wrapping and preserving so many bones, Edward's attention to the site paid off. The *Allosaurus* skeleton would be a triumph back east. Beyond that, as he suspected, the passage of so many millions of years would reduce metal and leather to it most basic components; but the process of preserving and sometimes transforming bone into stone could produce an unexplainable paradox.

While chipping and dust-brooming stone fragments from the next layer of the site, Edward encountered what he had unconsciously expected. It marked the sole reason he had remained on-site. And as of this day, he would declare the 1876 expedition at an end, because of what his obsessive paleontological techniques had afforded him. Amidst the bones of a creature who walked the earth one hundred fifty million years ago, Edward uncovered what simply could *not* be there, what no one else could ever know: the skull of a nineteenth-century human.

Its right front incisor still gleamed with immutable gold.

ACKNOWLEDGMENTS

This one would have never been written without the urgings and encouragement of Tony & Tori Eldridge, the patience of Jonathan Maberry, the acumen of Lane Heymont, and the infinite wisdom of Christopher C. Payne.

Everyone—*grazie mille!*

ABOUT THE AUTHOR

THOMAS F. MONTELEONE has published more than 100 short stories, 5 collections, 9 anthologies and 30 novels—including the *NY Times* bestseller and *New York Times* Notable Book of the Year, *The Blood of the Lamb*. A five-time winner of the Bram Stoker Award, he's also written scripts for stage, screen, and TV, as well as the bestselling *The Complete Idiot's Guide to Writing a Novel* (now in a 2nd edition). His latest novels are a global thriller, *Submerged,* and the conclusion of a YA trilogy, *The Silent Ones* (with F. Paul Wilson). With his daughter, Olivia, he co-edits the award-winning anthology series of imaginative fiction—*Borderlands.* With his wife, Elizabeth, he is a co-founder of Borderlands Press as well as the annual Borderlands Press Writers Boot Camp. He is well-known as an entertaining reader of his work, and routinely draws a large, appreciative audience at conventions. Despite being dragged kicking and screaming into his seventies and losing most of his hair, he still thinks he is dashingly handsome—humor him. In the spring of 2017, he received the Lifetime Achievement Award from the Horror Writers Association at StokerCon in Long Beach California.

www.ingramcontent.com/pod-product-compliance
Lightning Source LLC
Chambersburg PA
CBHW032206190626
46810CB00018B/1892